Simon's Island

The rocks looked securely fixed, but Simon began to pull on one that protruded more than the others. He looked carefully at the stones wedged round it, afraid they might subside and crush the animals as they fell inside. Or he might bring rock on to his own head.

Reason told him he was being stupid, but the sharp insistent bark below him spurred him on. The rock twisted under his hands and slid away so suddenly that he shot through the gap, falling an incredible distance, sliding down the slope. He landed with a jerk that sickened him and looked forlornly up at the sky that showed so far above him.

Simon's Island

Joyce Stranger

with illustrations by
David O'Conner

Collins

An imprint of HarperCollins Publishers

First published in Great Britain by Collins in 1996
Collins is an imprint of
HarperCollins*Publishers* Ltd, 77–85 Fulham Palace Road,
Hammersmith, London W6 8JB

1 3 5 7 9 8 6 4 2

Copyright © Joyce Stranger 1996

ISBN 0 00 675136 9

The author asserts the moral right to be identified
as the author of the work.

Printed and bound in Great Britain
by HarperCollins Manufacturing Ltd, Glasgow

To my friend Angela
and of course her goldies –
Katie, and her daughters,
Emma and Shona –
and Lisa who came back to
her breeder after this book
was written – she'd hate to
be forgotten.

CHAPTER 1

He was trying to run, but his legs were weighted. He could hear the pounding footsteps behind him, the mocking yells. They were as familiar to him as his own voice. They had tormented him for the whole of this first year at his new school.

He was small for his age and his tormentors were lumping giants, clumsy, hard-fisted, with eyes that feasted on his fear. They grew in stature as he looked at them and he felt diminished. They were cunning, and no one ever saw them trap him.

They knew every turn in the road on his way home. They knew where he waited for the school bus. They knew when he would appear through the gate of his home. They knew when his brother would be with him and then they never even cast a look in his direction.

"If you tell . . .", they said, as they robbed him of his pocket money and lunch. He was never sure if it was worse to carry nothing, or to have something that would appease their greed. He turned a corner and there was a blank wall and they were on him. He screamed, and woke.

He was shaking with fear still, sweat pouring off his face. An owl called, softly, insistently, and then followed a long barking. Fox? He wondered, not knowing. Everything here was strange. He missed the street lamp that shone across his ceiling and the sounds of voices and of passing cars. He switched on the light and looked at his watch. 3 a.m. He was afraid to go back to sleep, afraid to dream again.

He was here at his grandparents' home on the west coast of Scotland because he had been ill, but was almost better. He had had glandular fever, which was very nasty, and had been in bed for a long time, his glands swollen, his head aching, and with no strength at all.

Those dreams haunted him and haunted the whole family as he screamed in terror. The doctor thought the nightmares would vanish if he went away, and spent the rest of the summer term recovering.

They didn't vanish. Tonight was the worst he had had. When people asked him what he had dreamed about all he could answer was "I don't remember", because he was too afraid of Them. They had names that he hid in his mind. Crocker, and Peterson, and Smith.

He was Simon McGregor. A name to be proud of, his father always said. The three called him Simple Simon and urged the other children in the playground to sing silly songs after him.

"Simple Simon met a pieman
  Going to the fair."

It was silly to mind, but he did mind. He hated maths too as he found it very difficult and the teacher was impatient. "Simple Simon never gets anything right," he said one day. The name stuck. Simple Simon.

Simple. Simple. Simple. The children shouted it after him, laughing at him.

He could make himself feel sick just thinking of it. If only he were as big as his brother, who towered above them. They would never dare tease Hamish, even if they did find his name hilarious. The McGregor brothers were the only Scottish children in the school.

They teased Evan Price too, with his Welsh accent, calling after him "Taffy was a Welshman", but Evan had a temper that flared in a second and fists that hit like small hailstones. He waded into his tormentors, yelling at the top of his voice, which always brought someone to his rescue. Simon couldn't yell. Nor could he hit back. Nor had he the words to use to quell his enemies.

Simple Simon's a wimp.

Why was he so afraid of everything and everyone? Other boys weren't. Or they hid it well. Maybe if he pretended to find it funny they'd leave him alone, but he couldn't pretend. He couldn't overcome the dread that they roused in him, and if he did find words, he found them long after, in the middle of the night, when the opportunity had long gone.

There were so many things that worried him. When he was worried he couldn't work well, couldn't remember and when Mr Wolfe pointed a long thin finger at him and said, "Let's have an answer from Simple

9

Simon," the words dried up in his mouth and he couldn't even speak and the whole class laughed and Mr Wolfe with them. He was well named.

The only time he was really happy was with Mr Longton who taught English and who loved poetry and loved words.

"There's magic in words," he said. "They can flash and they can flame and they can flare. They can linger, they can dawdle, they can drop like a heavy stone. They can be light and lilting and dancing and entrancing, or they can sound like the boom of a far waterfall."

Then he had read them Hilaire Belloc's poem, which began, "Do you remember an inn, Miranda, do you remember an inn?"

Simon couldn't remember all of it but snatches from it sang to him; the whirl and the twirl of the girl gone dancing; the fleas that tease in the high Pyrenees and the wine that tasted of tar; the cheers and the jeers of the young muleteers. The hip hop hap of the hands that clap . . . The fast beat as the words flew, and then the change in rhythm, and the inn had gone. Never more, Miranda, never more, only the high peaks hoar . . . As Mr Longton read, the words dropped icily, like stones.

There was magic in poetry and in the books that Mr Longton introduced him to, written by writers who loved their craft, who made each word meaningful, who could spin enchantment, and carry him away to the moon, or a distant country, or another time, so that he could forget his worries.

He began to recite to himself, saying the words

10

softly, under his breath, trying to remove the memory of his dream.

"The woods are lovely, dark and deep, but I have promises to keep, and miles to go before I sleep." He was with the poet on his pony, the woodlands magical, a clear cold moon shining.

He was startled when his door opened.

"I saw your light," Grandmother McGregor said. She looked unfamiliar, her grey hair rumpled into tiny curls. By day she was usually so neat. A long blue dressing gown was caught round her waist with a plaited cord.

"You couldn't sleep? Neither could I. I heard the fox barking and wondered if he were after the hens, so went to look. Your grandfather never hears anything in the night, but it only needs a sound from the beasts and I'm wide awake. I expect the fox woke you."

She sat in the wicker chair which creaked whenever anyone moved. Simon wondered if his parents had told her about the dreams. Nobody ever mentioned them in this house. He had been here three weeks already. He saw Dr McLeod every week and every week Dr McLeod said he needed more time to get his strength back, though he felt as strong as he ever had. He was only just beginning to want to eat. Glandular fever went on for ages.

"Must be strange for you here," Grandmother said, looking at him thoughtfully, her blue eyes more vivid than ever. "I hate towns. They always seem so crowded and so dirty."

"I never thought about it," Simon said. "It's so quiet here. And so big and the mountains shut us in on one side, and the moors go on for ever on the other. It's scary."

"It's wonderful," Grandmother said, laughing at him. "You can run and shout and scream and throw stones in the sea, and nobody cares. You can grow your own food and rear your own sheep and milk your own cows, and fish for your dinner, and it's all there for the taking. No need to worry about running out. There's Leila brimming over with milk for us, and I can make butter and cream and cheese. My bread is better than any of your shop-bought pap, and there's eggs from the hens every morning."

Simon thought about her words. His grandfather had been a fisherman first and then a crofter. The cottage where they lived had had extensions added over the years and was now much larger than when they first bought it. His grandmother, who loved horses, bred hardy little Shetland ponies which she sold for children to ride.

"It's lonely," Simon said.

"Maybe a bit now," his grandmother agreed. "Just Duncan left and he's away to college soon. But when all ten bairns were home it was far from lonely, believe me. We had birthday parties all the time with twelve of us, and then Christmas and Easter and Harvest Festival. There were Sunday School outings and picnics and the Scouts and the Guides. We were busy people then, even if we did live at the far end of nowhere. You ask your father. He'll remember, even if he has been long gone, the oldest of our bairns."

It was odd to think of his tall father as a child, living in this home, a baby, then a little boy, a Cub and then a Scout. Growing up as Simon was growing up, going to school and coming home again.

Simon had a sudden vision of the cottage filled with all ten aunts and uncles, with his father the eldest, and Duncan the youngest by over twenty years, only six years older than Simon himself. Not like an uncle at all, but more like an older brother.

"Feel like sleeping now?" his grandmother asked.

Simon looked into his own mind and saw a vision of the nightmare recurring.

"I'm wide awake," he said.

"Then on with that nice warm dressing gown your mother bought for you, and your slippers, and we'll have a midnight feast." She laughed. "I haven't done that for years. It'll be fun." Simon grinned, feeling as if they were in deepest intrigue together.

He loved the big kitchen with the Aga that warmed the whole house and the big shabby armchair in which Cleo, the tortoiseshell cat, was curled sleeping. She mewed indignantly when Grandmother lifted her and put her on the floor and her eyes glared at Simon when he sat in the chair.

"There are things I thank civilization for," Grandmother said, foraging in the refrigerator and producing milk and two little round pasties. "Like electricity, though we've only had that for four years. Cost a fortune to put in. We had Calor gas before that, but it meant a lot of fetching and carrying."

She put the pasties on two plates and began to heat the milk to make cocoa.

"I'm quite sure I'll be in trouble, giving you pastry in the middle of the night. Give you nightmares."

I don't need pastry to give me those, Simon thought. He glanced at the clock. He'd never been up in the middle of the night to eat a feast. His mother would have a fit if she knew what he was doing. She thought the night was for sleeping and anyone who didn't sleep needed treatment.

"I don't sleep well now I'm old," Grandmother said. "Better to get up and do something than lie awake fretting and listening to your grandfather snoring and sleeping the sleep of the just."

"What do you do when I'm not here?" Simon asked.

"There's always plenty to do. I might get dressed, and go out and clean the byre; or go and talk to the pigs. Or take a walk down to the loch and look at the water, shining silver in the moonlight, silver everywhere, where the water creams against the shore, and the fish arrow through the waves. The night is beautiful."

Simon suddenly remembered another of Mr Longton's poems. "Crouched in his kennel, like a log, with paws of silver sleeps the dog." He said the words aloud.

"So you like poetry too. Good. There's nothing like it, though I don't much care for the modern stuff they produce. I like rhyme and wonderful words. *Daffodils*. That one gave your grandfather an idea for my silver wedding present; he planted a sea of daffodils and I never knew till they came through, nearly on the right day. A great sweep of them in front of the cottage going down to the sea. You must come in daffodil time. It's a wonderful sight."

Simon ate the last crumb of his pasty. It was the first time for weeks that he had really enjoyed his food. Maybe the feeling of doing something unusual had helped.

"Away to your bed. Up we go, lad." She stacked the plates and mugs and put them in the sink to wash in the morning.

Simon thought of his dream, and felt a catch in his throat.

"I'm not tired," he said. "I don't feel like going to bed."

"Then we won't," Grandmother said. "Go and put on your jeans and a thick jersey and an anorak over your pyjamas. Hat as well, it's chilly outside. We'll go adventuring."

Simon dressed hastily and ran down again, careful not to make a noise. His grandmother was also dressed, a knitted cap with a pompom on it on her head.

Outside the moon was full, sliding down the sky, and the brilliant stars blazed above him. He followed his grandmother down to the edge of the loch, and they balanced carefully on a shelf of rock overlooking the water.

The waves glittered as they broke against the shore. Fish streaked through the water. Simon leaned over and dipped his hand into the cold sea, and watched as light sparkled in bands all around him, light slipped from his fingers, drop after shimmering drop.

He had forgotten the dogs. Katie, the second oldest of his grandfather's golden retrievers, had followed them, and she also watched, her head on one side, as if she too were fascinated. She sat beside Simon, leaning against his leg, her warm body hard and muscular.

He stroked her with his wet hand and beads of light shone on her coat.

"What is it?" he asked, awed by the display.

"A tiny creature that is in millions in the sea; it's phosphorescent and gives off light. You don't often see it like this. We've been lucky. Some nights we all go fishing and the oars glisten, the wake behind us glows, and our lines are ashiver with light where they enter the sea and the fish we catch gleam like ghosts."

"It's magic," Simon said, and was suddenly caught by a tremendous yawn.

"Time for sleep," Grandmother said firmly, and Simon followed Katie back to the cottage.

Lying in bed, when the door was shut and the light was out, Simon thought how unexpected people were. He had had no idea that his grandmother loved poetry too or that Grandfather had the imagination to make a forest of daffodils as a present for his wife.

He tried to imagine them in the springtime massing all the way to the edge of the loch, a great sea of yellow, to meet the glimmering water on a moony night. Did it glow when there was no moon? That must be even more spectacular.

He fell asleep, and slept without dreaming. He woke, eager and excited, feeling well for the first time for weeks, and dressed quickly, remembering that Duncan had promised to take him fishing.

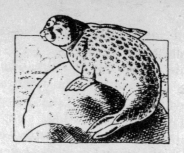

CHAPTER 2

"Look!" Simon was entranced, afraid to shout in case the seal and her baby vanished. The two animals were watching the boat intently, heads projecting, wise-eyed, from the dappled water. The sun shone, a little wind ruffled the wave tops and a cormorant stood on a nearby rock, spreading its wings to the warmth.

The fibreglass dinghy nosed its way across the loch, dancing lightly over a multi-coloured surface: ultramarine, dark cobalt blue, and in places a clear deep green, transparent as glass, so that they could look down to the sea bed, watching fish dive and dart. The white sandy shore was edged with black rock, partly covered in brilliant orange sea wrack, and at the water's edge the little waves broke in a flurry of foam.

The line streamed out from the reel, the spinner twisting in the sun. Tai, Duncan's Siamese cat that went everywhere with him, stretched out a lazy paw and tapped at Simon's hand. His blue eyes, slightly a-squint, watched the dip and dive of two terns,

17

spinning in the air. Purring, he settled on Duncan's knees and watched the seals.

The mother seal nosed her baby. The little head vanished, and a moment later the water was still, as if they had never been there.

"I never thought I'd be glad I had glandular fever," Simon said, hoping that the two heads would surface again. "Just think, nearly four weeks before I need go back to school and I've got you all to myself. Sheena and Hamish are jealous." Sheena was his younger sister.

Simon at twelve was small for his age. Duncan, now eighteen, was as big as Simon's father, Duncan's eldest brother, though not nearly so solid. Both Simon and his uncle had brown eyes and dark hair and a skin that owed its colour to a long-ago Spanish ancestor, who had been marooned when the Armada came to grief.

Duncan, holding the tiller of the little outboard motor, laughed as Tai yowled loudly. There had been a twitch on Simon's line.

"That cat knows more than you do about fishing," he said, stretching out his hand to rub Tai behind the ears. There was a deafening purr. "He's as clever as any dog."

The cat loved the boat. He told them every time they hooked a mackerel, knowing that they needed to remove the fish. His ear-splitting squawk sounded oddly out there on the water. The cat also knew that in due course he would have a tasty meal from their catch.

Simon tested the line. It was dancing vigorously and he was not sure at first whether he had really hooked a mackerel or had become entangled in seaweed.

A fish leaped high, attempting to break free, landed heavily and dashed away from the boat. The line was alive, tugging, twisting, spinning fast off the reel. Simon braked. The fish fought against the pull that brought it slowly closer to the dinghy. It began to tire. Its struggles were less strong and Simon reeled in. Tai, eager, watched expectantly, and sniffed as the fish came aboard. He tapped at the lashing tail with a tentative paw.

Duncan killed it with a sharp tap on the head, and removed Tai.

"You'll eat it cooked, not raw," he told the cat, who stared at him and yowled his loud Siamese cry. "He makes enough noise to wake the dead," Duncan added, and Tai weaved round his legs, knowing that everyone loved him.

It was the third fish they had caught that afternoon. The mackerel were shoaling and the edge of the loch was alive with tiny fish, no bigger than small shrimps, that had fled into shallow water to escape the barred predators that feasted on them.

"Time to go," Duncan said. "I promised your gran that I wouldn't keep you out too long. That was a nasty dose of fever."

It was odd to think that Simon's gran was Duncan's mother. Soon Duncan would be off to college, studying to be a doctor. Simon hoped he wouldn't be too grown up then to want to take his nephew out fishing. He stretched cramped arms and legs and pushed the dark strands of straight hair away from his eyes. He eased clenched sun-tanned fingers. The weather had been kind in the weeks that he had been in Scotland.

19

He felt better than he had for months, and he also felt safe, although at times he was worried by the fear that the boat might overturn and land them in the water, or that lightning would strike out of a blue sky. He wished he was brave. He envied Duncan, who never seemed to be afraid of anything. Maybe he wouldn't either when he was eighteen.

A heron brooded at the water's edge, growing fat on the fry that seethed in the shallows. Its grey body was still until the long sharp beak flashed down swiftly and the bird lifted its head to swallow. The wind ruffled the dark crest of feathers upon its crown. The beak stabbed the water again.

It walked forward, a stately bird, and Duncan leaned across the boat and nudged Simon.

'Look!'

The bird had been hiding two young herons. The shoaling mackerel out in the loch had driven the small fry into the edge of the water, seeking safety from the greedy horde. The two little herons were entranced, their beaks stabbing down again and again into the seething mass of little fish that frothed at the edge of the foam.

They had long ceased to be hungry. They were glutted from the feast. The tiny silvery bodies piled up beside them, as they went on fishing for the sheer pleasure of the act.

There was a cry across the loch and the adult bird answered, winging slowly across the wave tops, calling to her youngsters. Neither heard. They were obsessed. The heron called again and a second bird flew towards her, his legs almost touching the water. The first bird turned, and together they flew back to the beach and to their erring young. Quite suddenly both the little ones were startled by their parents' wings and beaks beating at them, scolding them for their misbehaviour, driving them into the air.

Duncan grinned at Simon.

"Who'd have believed that?" he asked. "Evidently little birds can be as naughty as small boys. Just look at that heap of fish there on the beach."

"Wasted," Simon said, regretfully.

"Oh no. Watch."

Within minutes the gulls were overhead, screaming, diving, grabbing at the booty which had saved them so much energy. They squawked and squabbled, and occasionally two birds rose on the air, breast to breast, stabbing beaks at one another.

"Pirates," Duncan said. Tai, who had been watching with fascination, yowled.

Far across the loch a large dinghy made its way towards the island, the outboard motor noisy. Tai yowled.

"Are they neighbours?" Simon asked.

"I've never seen that boat before." Duncan laughed. "Maybe they're smugglers. This place was famous – or infamous – once, and the island was supposed to be a smuggler's hideout." He looked at Simon's worried face. "It doesn't happen now. They'll be fishing, like us. Probably holiday-makers."

Simon put away his rod and looked about him. At the water, surrounded by mountains down which pine trees marched in endless procession; at the rocky beach where hoodie crows turned over the brown-gold sea wrack, searching for food; at the sky where black clouds streaked with scarlet laced with eggshell-green and golden streaks pointed to the setting sun. A chaffinch, brighter than any city bird, flashed among the bushes bordering the shore.

"Wind tonight," Duncan said, looking up at the sky. He pointed. "See those streamers? The wind'll come in the early dawn and tomorrow it will blow too hard for fishing. You'll see."

Simon wished he knew as much as Duncan. It was much more fun here than at home so long as he was not alone. Home was in a suburb, with a ginger cat and two hamsters. Here the wide open spaces frightened him. The moors seemed to stretch for ever, into emptiness, and very few people ever called.

The nights were uncanny, without the noise of traffic as a constant reminder of the busy motorway within ten minutes' walk. No street outside with people passing, no sound of hurrying footsteps, of voices calling, of car doors slamming. No weekend sounds of electric drills and mowing machines, and neighbours chatting over garden fences.

Here there was the cow Leila and her new calf; Moke, the old donkey, bought at a sale for five pounds, old and lame, but now happy in his retirement. There were hardy mountain sheep, and chickens and geese and ducks, and the horses and ponies. Sentinel, the big gander, marched up to the cottage door every morning and banged on it with his beak, demanding a slice of bread.

There were Grandfather's four golden retrievers:

Jansen the old man, nearly thirteen, slow and stately, dreaming by the fire, and solemn six-year-old Katie, who took her motherhood seriously. Grandmother had kept two of the pups. Emma, from her first litter, and Shona from the second. Maybe if she had a third, Simon might have a puppy to take home. He dreamed of having his own dog.

Today, safe with Duncan, the world bathed in the late sunshine which brightened the moors and lochs and hills, he did not mind the space all round him. He grinned at his companion, overcome with pleasure too deep for words.

He was beginning to enjoy himself. The sea worried him when the wind was fierce but today was as calm as his bath water, and there was no threat anywhere.

All the same, he avoided going out alone, and clung to his young uncle, hoping Duncan would not realize his fear.

Two days earlier the wind had screamed round the cottage, and the electricity had failed. The darkness was an enemy. He had never known a power cut in the town where he lived, other than for a few minutes and then in daylight. The candle light was slightly spooky, as were the many shadows that flickered in the corners and the wild cries that Duncan said were herons in their nests, frightened by the wind that bowed the trees almost to ground level.

Today it was hard to realize the savagery that had blown the roof off part of the barn and felled a giant tree. He glanced up at the sky, already learning to read the signs of bad weather threatening them but the sun continued to shine out of a cloudless blue arc, and light glinted on the ripples. He glanced out to the centre of the loch, to the little island.

"Smugglers' Island," he said, savouring the sound of the words that conjured up silent men rowing with muffled oars, horses with their hooves padded to hide the sound, brandy kegs and lace, all hidden at night. He didn't mind smugglers so long as they belonged to the past. Rumour told of Black Douglas, who had lived there long ago, far from the haunts of the Preventive Men who chased the smugglers in more populous places. His house was a ruin now, its crumbling roofless walls stark against the sky. "Can we go there some day?"

"Perhaps," Duncan said. "Tomorrow we might be going salmon fishing, if the weather holds, but I doubt if it will. We own the fishing rights on the river, and try to catch what we want to eat."

It was a long way from the cottage, tucked under a crag by the side of Loch Arran, to the nearest shops. The McGregors and their neighbours lived off the land and the loch.

They had fed, that week, on trout and mackerel, on omelettes and freshly picked mushrooms, on peas and beans that his grandfather grew and his grandmother froze. Chickens and turkey came from a neighbour, as did pork and lamb and beef, all exchanged for trout and salmon and mackerel and sea bass, which formed a good part of their catch. His grandfather caught them in the surf off the rocks.

Simon was learning to respect the sea, which could be soft and smooth as silk, and then a few hours later, a roaring monster, crashing on the beaches, raging as it broke in flurries of white foam that were flung into the air and tossed on the wind so that everything tasted of salt.

The sea brought them much of their food. Nobody had been to a shop since Simon arrived, except to buy stamps to put on his letters home. Grandmother had to be much more organized than his mother who could just send Hamish, Simon or Sheena down the road if they ran out of sugar or butter. Life was so different here. Simon never knew what would happen next.

Only that morning, as they set out for the boat, he had seen a hare run through the furrow, and then pause and sit. It had been raining and the little animal perched on its hind legs, wringing water from its ears, taking first one and then the other between its two front paws and squeezing, much as his sister squeezed the water out of her hair with a towel when she washed it.

"None of your friends will have seen that," Duncan had said.

Simon felt a small germ of confidence grow in him. His three enemies from school had never visited a place like this. He knew things they would never know.

He looked briefly up to the cottage as they drew near to the shore, remembering his night-time fears, which seemed absurd in daylight. They had taken lunch to eat on the water, but he was hungry again, longing for his evening meal. He wanted to tell Duncan of his midnight exploration, but he had promised grandmother that he would keep it a secret. They pulled the boat on to the beach, making it safe.

Duncan took the outboard motor while Simon carried their rods and the fish. Tai marched behind them, his tail in the air, occasionally leaving them to inspect a tussock or clump of grass in the hope it might shelter a mouse. He loved walking with them, and often came with the dogs.

"Why are the birds so noisy?" Simon asked, aware of a constant chatter and din from every bush and tree.

"They're warning one another. Cat, cat, cat. I can always tell when Tai is coming home if he's been out hunting on his own as the bird calls come closer and closer, following him. It's a very efficient early warning system. Listen when you go home. You'll find your birds tell you when Ginger is coming."

That night they fed on grilled mackerel, and home-grown jacket potatoes, tiny peas that were sweeter than any bought at home and raspberries from the freezer, topped with lashings of cream from Leila.

"I'll get fat," Simon said, enjoying every mouthful. He had had no appetite at all when he arrived.

"You'll grow bonny, instead of looking like a plucked chicken they've forgotten to feed," his grandmother said and heaped more raspberries and cream on to his plate.

The moon came up, full and low, lighting the hills and casting long shadows. Duncan took Simon out into the night, pointing out the Plough and the Dog Star, Orion and the Great Bear.

Next day was as windy as Duncan had predicted. Grandfather decided to take a day off work and walk with them. The dogs ran ahead, delighted to be free to explore the undergrowth and find enticing smells that told them what creatures had run across the ground. They went towards the loch, heads bowed to keep the rain from their eyes. They sheltered behind an old shepherd's bothy, where once the men had slept when the ewes were lambing.

Wind whipped the water to a frenzied froth, and sang in the wires that brought electricity to the croft. That had come four years before, when they built the windmill farm. The giant machines dominated the edge of the nearest mountain. Eyesores, Grandmother said, but she welcomed the ability to have electric light, a vacuum cleaner and the two deep freezes that enabled them to stock up for weeks instead of having to trek frequently to the shops. There were so many benefits that the windpower brought.

"The marsh is a nature reserve," Grandfather said, pointing to the spit of land that jutted into the loch. "There are all kinds of rare things there. I found a man orchid last year, a weird little whitey yellow plant with flowers that look like the head and two legs of a man. And there are all kinds of rare butterflies as well. There's an osprey's nest in the big tree. That's a secret. No one knows and we don't want anyone to find out, or they'll steal the eggs. I heard the youngsters squalling for food early this year."

There had been an osprey fishing on the loch the day before, a huge bird with its feathered legs and cruel bill. It dived and caught a trout far more easily than Simon had caught his mackerel. It stood on a rock, the wild fish tail thrashing across its face, and then managed to stun the fish by slamming it against the hard surface.

A cormorant sailed across the water, fighting the wind. Its legs trailed the wave tops. It lifted slowly and flew off, its heavy humped shoulders dark against the lowering sky.

"Over there, where the water's white, are rocks that show only at low tide," Grandfather said. "A place to avoid like the plague when you're in a boat. There's a rip tide and eddies, and a fast undertow that has taken several swimmers and killed them. You can never take liberties with boats. Or mountains. This is a sea loch, remember. Out at sea, waves breaking may be a sign of rocks, or of sandbanks. Both are bad for sailors."

They walked on, along paths that were memories of the days when this had been a great estate. The huge old house was roofless now, the walls gaping open to let in wind and rain, the floors rotted, the windows long gone. Swallows nested in the deserted rooms, swooping in and out of the empty window frames.

Duncan pointed out the remains of their nests. They stared in at empty windows, at deserted rooms, the floors leaf-covered. The wind sang eerily through the cracks and round the corners, and one door, still hanging, swung to and fro in the gale. Once the path had led to a jetty, but this too was only a memory, its girders standing stark from the surging water, the slipway overgrown and dangerous with dark slimy weed.

Simon thought of the men who had once lived there, the laird in his greystone house, owning all the land for miles around, and the steward on the windy hill, his house also empty now, the uncurtained windows looking out over shadowed mountain and rippled loch.

They were well protected from the rain by oilskins that crackled as they walked. Tai hated rain and stayed at home, occasionally running to either the front or the back door, convinced that humans could turn off this awful weather if they only tried and complaining bitterly because they wouldn't.

They took a path that led through the once beautiful gardens, now overgrown and wild, hiding many woodland creatures. A weasel started from the bushes as they approached, a baby rabbit in its mouth. It vanished in thick undergrowth.

"You want to talk to Old John Macdonald at the garage," Grandfather said. "His father was coachman to the laird. In those days the drive was rolled and sanded every day, and the stables were full of horses: horses for the ladies to ride, for the men to hunt, to pull carriage and coach and gig and governess cart, ponies for the children. There were wrought iron gates between the pillars over there, and the badge of the family was an owl, the motto Tempus Fugit."

"What does that mean?" Simon asked.

"Time flies," Duncan said. "It does too. We ought to be turning back or we'll be late for our evening meal and that's a major sin." Lunch had been a picnic, of fresh-baked rolls filled with cheese and home-made chutney, of fruit cake and apples that grew on a tree outside the cottage.

Simon felt as if they had walked for miles, but this was a healthy tiredness, not the overwhelming exhaustion he had felt a few days before when he crawled miserably into bed wondering if he'd be able to get up again in the morning.

They were in dense woodland that had once been planted with cedar, cyprus and laburnum. The overgrown drive was bordered by yew, and there were monkey puzzles and Spanish chestnuts, and trees from Africa and the Lebanon, as well as blue spruces. One tree blazed with red and gold leaves, that seemed to shine even in the rain. Another was a fiery yellow.

A squirrel sitting on a bough chattered angrily at them.

"Red squirrel. You don't often see those. The greys have driven them out in most places, which is a shame." Duncan was admiring the tiny beast.

Simon looked at a palm tree.

"I thought those only grew in the tropics," he said.

"The Gulf Stream runs round this coast," Grandfather answered. "It's quite warm in winter. Nothing like the frosts that you get at home."

The rain had stopped, and there was a faint glint of sun. They walked through long coarse grass, and Simon was suddenly uneasily aware that something was stalking them. There was a crashing sound in the bushes, but nothing could be seen.

Duncan caught his arm.

"Stand still," he said.

"What is it?"

"I don't know."

"A badger?"

"Much too big. It can't be a deer. They're far too timid to stalk us, and I think that's what it's doing."

He looked uneasily around him. Even Grandfather looked worried.

Simon had a vision of a prowling tiger, ready to leap on them. It could have escaped from a circus. There were rumours of a great black beast that prowled at night and tore the throats from sheep. He gripped Duncan's hand and they stood, listening.

"Nothing. Come on."

The noise began again as soon as they started walking. Stop and it stopped.

"Doesn't seem to be coming near us," Grandfather said, but he spoke too soon. They came to a clearing, and there was a sudden flurry of movement as a huge black shape sped towards them, its feet thundering on the hard ground.

CHAPTER 3

Simon's throat was dry. This was worse than any of his
nightmares, or even the events that provoked them.
He took a deep breath, not wanting Duncan to see
how scared he was.

The creature speeding towards them was a monster
from the depths of hell, an unbelievable animal, without a head. There was a deep depression in its back, as
if a saddle had been cut from it. Simon gasped in
terror, and Duncan stared and then began to laugh.

The beast reached them, braked, and snuffled.
Close to, Simon saw a black horse with a greyish-white
head and greyish-white saddle marking on its body.
These had merged with the dusk to give the most
extraordinary appearance. The big head with its liquid
brown eyes rubbed against Duncan, greeting an old
friend.

"Fidget, you old ass, you scared us silly," Duncan
said, dipping into his pocket and producing two pep-
permints, which were accepted with soft lips. "No
sugar today. Who'd expect to see you?" The ears

moved backwards and forwards as if the horse were trying to understand the words. He certainly knew about sugar.

Duncan began to walk on, the horse plodding companionably beside him.

"He isn't one of Gran's?" Simon asked. It was a question, not a statement.

"He was," Duncan said. "He's old; nearly thirty and Mum thought it would be better for him to have a quieter life, instead of trying to romp with the younger horses. So she gave him to Jock McIntosh, who used to be a lighthouse keeper at Bray Point. The old man's been lonely since he retired."

"I'd have thought lighthouse-keeping was lonely," Simon said, remembering the stark rock far out at sea that was Bray Point.

"Ah, but there were three of them. Now he lives by himself and his cottage is fairly isolated. The horse gave him something to do. We'll have to persuade old Fidget to go back to his new home. Jock'll be upset at losing him." Grandfather patted Fidget on his nose. "You silly old thing. You don't know when you're well off."

"Why Fidget?" Simon asked. The cottage was in sight, the lights bright and welcoming, spilling out across the garden that was his grandmother's delight.

"He'd never stand still for his harness as a youngster He was a pain, fidgeting from one hoof to the other, stamping and tossing his head to avoid the bridle, snorting and carrying on. Used to drive us all up the wall."

They turned into the yard. Tai yowled, greeting the

33

dogs, pleased to be home. The sound of hooves on cobbles brought Simon's grandmother to the door.

"Where did he come from?" she asked, looking in amazement at the horse.

"Found us in the woods and scared us silly," Duncan said, laughing again. "We couldn't see his head or his saddle in the gloom and he looked a right odd shape; a headless monster. I think Simon thought we were being chased by a demon."

"We'll have to ring Jock. He'll be worried." She walked over to the horse who neighed in recognition and rubbed his head hard against her shoulder. "You old goose, were you missing us? Maybe you'll be happier if I send Bracken with you. They were always good friends," she added to Simon, who was somewhat astonished by the ways of horses. "Bracken is twenty now; she won't get the old boy running too fast, racing with her against the wind as the youngsters do. He hates being left behind. You can take them both in the horsebox tomorrow, Duncan. Simon will enjoy Cairn Cottage, and old Jock is an education in himself."

Duncan led the horse to one of the stables, and filled the manger with hay.

"He thinks he's come home to stay, poor old fellow," he said. "He's travelled over twelve miles. Goodness knows how he found his way. He must be exhausted."

Simon's grandfather gave Fidget a carrot.

"It's sad when they get old," he said. "Have to give them a quieter life, but they don't understand. They still hear the old battle cries and the calls to arms, and think they're as young as they ever were."

Tai, always needing to be involved with everything that went on, walked into the stable and jumped on to the rug which Duncan had put on the horse's back. He curled up and was almost immediately asleep.

"He always did like sleeping there. Horses are not the only ones who won't accept old age," Simon's grandmother said. "I could tell many stories . . . "

"You can do a lot if the will's still there," Grandfather McGregor said, leading the way back to the kitchen. "People sometimes give up. Animals don't." He smiled as his old golden retriever, Jansen, stretched himself and rose stiffly from the rug in front of the fire. He plodded thoughtfully across the room and picked up a remarkably ragged woolly penguin, a relic of Duncan's young days and brought it to them in his mouth, his dark gold curly-coated body swaggering.

"Like old Jansen here. I took him to a little dog show a couple of years back and entered him in one of the classes for Obedience. He'd been retired three years before, but as soon as he got in the ring up went his head, and he seemed to shed years. Just like an old warhorse hearing the bugle sound, or a retired hunter hearing the horn. We won that class. There's the cup on the mantelpiece." Simon looked at it, a silver cup with elegant handles, in pride of place of the shelf. "Jansen's last fling. He was eleven years old then. He's nearly thirteen now."

Jansen had been there on every visit since Simon was born. He couldn't imagine the cottage without him. Katie was now the working dog and she greeted them in her turn, carrying her own toy, a woolly

35

tortoise wearing a knitted hat. Behind her, in procession, came her daughters, Emma, who was eighteen months old, and her six-month-old sister. Shona was a baby still and had everything to learn.

Grandfather trained his own dogs for the gun and hated other people exercising them or playing with them. "Spoil them for ever," he said.

They were jumping round the room, getting under everyone's feet, delighted to be home and pestering Grandmother for their meal.

"That's enough. Good dogs," Grandfather said, and the four dogs lay down on the hearth rug, their tails still beating. Jansen watched every move that the humans made. Katie and Emma played a small game in which Emma took her mother's mouth in her own, grunting slightly, and Shona, still fluffy with her puppy coat, rolled on to her back and lay with her legs in the air, blissful, the fire warming her tummy.

"Spoiled beasts. Time I was building that kennel for them," Grandfather said. He had been threatening to build the kennel for the last twenty years.

"I went fishing very early this morning, while you lazy creatures were all still asleep." He led them to the table. "Caught our supper." He smiled happily.

"Clean hands, Simon?" his grandmother asked, and he and Duncan went to wash. She followed them.

"That's funny. There was a plate of fish ready for the cats on the table. It's empty. None of them has been in here . . . " She stopped in mid-sentence. "That Tai. I left the back door open. I thought it was odd that he wasn't rooting round my heels asking for food. No wonder he felt sleepy. There was enough for five here. Short commons for him tomorrow and I'll have to use some of your mackerel, Duncan.

"We can still feast, though," she added. "Luckily I hadn't put ours out on the plates. It's still in the pan. Tai's the biggest thief we've ever had around here."

She produced salmon with parsley dressing, tiny peas, a cucumber salad and potatoes mashed with the milk in which the fish had been poached. They finished with loganberries, junket and cream. Simon adored his grandmother's food.

"Cooks like an angel," Grandfather often said and smiled at his wife. "The only reason I married her."

"The old wives always did say the only way to a man's heart is through his stomach." His wife smiled back at him. It was an often repeated joke and they never seemed to tire of it.

"I miss the old days," Grandmother said. "It's lovely to have you here, Simon. I hope Sheena and Hamish will come next year. It's three years since we saw them. The other grandchildren are all too little still to visit on their own and their parents are so busy. The house seems very empty now they've all left home. Donald in Australia and Eileen and Jeannie in America, so far away, and the others down in the south of England and such a long way to come." She sighed.

Simon had only met two of his aunts and had never met the uncle who had gone to Australia before he had been born. Their pictures were on the walls and on the bookcases. Wedding pictures, and photographs of small cousins he had never seen. A picture of his Aunt Moira in her doctor's gown, just after the graduation ceremony. A doctor, a vet, an engineer, and three school teachers. His own father worked as an accountant in a big factory making chemicals. Duncan was following in his elder sister's footsteps, training in medicine, though at a different college. Both his other uncles worked on the oil rigs.

The dogs did not move while they were at the table, but Cleo sat licking her lips, hoping that a morsel might fall to the floor, or even better that one of the humans would not be hungry and might leave a sizeable piece on the plate. Her four little kittens tumbled out of their basket and sat beside her, though they were not yet weaned. Tai slept on in the stable, far too full of food to wake and join them.

"Could we camp on Smugglers' Island?" Simon asked. He had always longed to sleep in a tent, but his mother hated camping and was sure they would meet all sorts of creepy crawlies, especially spiders, creatures that terrified her. Duncan often camped with his friends, cycling miles in the summer holidays. Simon had always envied him. It seemed such ages before he would be grown up too.

"Don't see why not, if the weather picks up. Have to wait a week or so, and make sure you're really fit again," Grandfather said, taking the salmon skin from the dish and cutting it into four, watched by the cats. He handed each a piece. Cleo took hers daintily, while the kittens snatched, though when they had their share they were not sure what to do with it.

Jansen barked.

"Your turn now," Grandfather said, and cut his bread roll into four pieces. He whistled and the four dogs came to sit in front of him, their eyes eager. Jansen put up his mouth and took the bread so softly that for a moment Simon was not sure whether the dog really had accepted the gift.

Katie put out her paw, and Grandfather shook it solemnly, then gave her her reward. Emma pushed at his leg.

"She never learns," he said. "Greedy girls come last."

Shona, as yet very young, put her paws on his knee and was told to sit still and behave. The two younger bitches sat, their eyes anxious. Were they going to be deprived?

"Emma." Emma came quietly, her tail waving very gently, unsure of her welcome. She took the bread as if she didn't quite believe her luck and went to the far side of the room lest Jansen took it from her.

Shona, sure she had been forgotten, whimpered forlornly and Grandfather patted her and smiled.

"Silly wee lass," he said. "Ye have to learn, like the others. There now, hush and eat up."

She too took her piece of bread away from her father and mother and sister and lay chewing.

"Time for the dogs to go out," Duncan said, walking to the outside door and opening it. There was a small explosion of bodies, which Grandfather quickly quelled. They stood at the door, waiting, and Duncan called each out in turn, Jansen, as always, first.

"He still keeps the girls in order," Grandfather said.

Outside the moon had ridden up the sky, and

shone full and clear, silvering grass and bushes and trees and glittering on water now smooth as patterned silk. The wind had died.

Jansen pawed at Duncan's leg, the air telling him of intruders. Duncan did not realize that he was being given important information and patted the old dog absent-mindedly. Jensen knew that a vixen had passed by, beyond the high garden wall, seeking sanctuary, hiding from men. She was slinking through the undergrowth, belly low to the ground and her ears flattened. She had a healed wound in her shoulder, where gunshot had grazed her, and hurt her for weeks. She had caught the scent of Duncan and Simon and was determined they would not detect her. Men meant danger. Men meant death.

There was a rumour on the wind from birds that were awake, telling of an enemy. Tai heard it and pricked his ears, but knew it was not about him. Cleo heard it and stayed indoors with her kittens as she had learned that there were animals more dangerous than cats abroad in the night. She had once met a vixen and had to run for her life.

Rabbit and hare took shelter. A weasel listened, one paw upraised and dived into his hole. An owl hooted, far away, and was answered from a nearby tree.

Fox, fox, fox, the warning cries said.

Jansen ran to the wall, his head in the air, sniffing, his nose working overtime. The other three followed him, all well aware that there was a stranger just beyond their territory. Katie barked once, and the vixen raced on.

Tai, scenting fox, jumped to the top of the wall,

leaped into the dense undergrowth and tracked her, curious. He was a big powerful cat, weighing a stone, much too large for a Siamese, according to the show people. His claws were long and sharp and he feared nothing. The vixen vanished, hidden in deep undergrowth, running fast for safety. Tai turned for home, and stalked a mouse, but was too full to bother to kill. The fish had been more than enough even for him, but he had been determined to eat every scrap. He followed the dogs indoors, and stretched himself on Duncan's bed to wait for his master.

Duncan went upstairs some time after Simon had fallen asleep in the little room under the eaves, just across the passage.

He began to sort out his camping gear. Tai watched, knowing that he too would be included as one of the first things that Duncan packed was the cat's warm rug and the feeding dish that was only used when they slept out of doors together. Tai was never allowed to follow when Duncan was on one of his cycling trips, and he resented being left at home. He always punished his master by ignoring him for a couple of weeks on his return.

Duncan had wondered if he might manage to find a basket that would strap on the carrier, but there was so much else to cart when he had the camping equipment too.

"I'll be away for weeks in a little while, when I start college," Duncan told the cat, who crawled up the duvet to curl against him when he finally went to bed. "I wish I could take you with me, but I can't and you wouldn't like it a bit, old son."

Tai, happy to be spoken to and not understanding a word, purred loudly, soothing his master to sleep. The vixen curled in her den to gather strength to hunt in the early dawn. At low tide she swam across the narrow strait to the island, hoping for more bounty there.

CHAPTER 4

"No camping until Fidget goes back," Grandmother said. "I rang Jock to say you'd bring him over, and Bracken with him. I can spare her, and the two are great friends. I think the old boy will settle if he isn't alone."

"How are we going to get them there?" Simon asked.

"Ride," Duncan answered. "We can't borrow the horsebox. Ian Campbell has taken some calves in it to market. I'll ride Bracken as she can be frisky but old Fidget is like an armchair."

"What about getting back? I can't walk twelve miles."

"Dad will come for us in the Land Rover. Jock's offered us lunch."

Simon, stuffing himself with egg, bacon, sausage and fried bread, as his grandmother was quite sure he needed building up, was very doubtful about the whole adventure. He had never been on a horse before. "I could easily fall off."

"I promise you won't," Duncan said, seeing his

43

expression. "Nobody could fall off Fidget and we'll only be walking. No fancy trotting or cantering."

"Suppose he bolts?"

"He won't bolt. Come on, you'll end up looking like a feather pillow if you eat any more and then your mum won't let you come again." Duncan was out of the room, Tai following, complaining loudly that nobody had yet given him his breakfast. Within seconds Cleo was with him, adding her noise to his. The kittens, not to be outdone, yelled too.

"Give a body a chance, can't you?" But his grandmother was laughing as she said it, busy dishing food on to all the small plates. A moment later there was silence.

Duncan fastened blankets on to the backs of both horses.

"No need for saddles," he said, and then laughed. "We don't have any, anyway, as none of us rides the horses. They're all retired. The blanket will make it a bit softer for us."

Simon looked dubiously at Fidget. His back looked a very long way off the ground.

"Just sit tight and hang on to his mane. He won't mind. If we need to go left you pull gently with your left hand, and to turn right use your right hand. It's as easy as falling off a log."

Simon wasn't sure he liked the sound of that either.

Jansen, following them, barked.

"Too far for you, old lad. You look after the youngsters. We'll take Katie. Do her good to have some peace and get away from her daughters for a bit." The old dog lay down, his nose on his paws, his eyes unhappy. "I'd love to take you, old fellow, but you couldn't make it," Duncan said, patting him, and leading him indoors.

When he came out again he jumped up on to Bracken's back and led the way out of the stable yard. Simon was afraid he might be left sitting on a horse that refused to move, but where Bracken went, Fidget went too, and he soon followed.

The wind had died and the sun was breaking through a thin cloud cover. Katie ran ahead of them, circled them, identifying wonderful scents on the ground and glorious smells in the trees. She found a chunky thick stick and decided to carry it, settling to walk alongside them, her tail waving merrily, her eyes bright with enjoyment.

After a few minutes Simon began to lose his fear and enjoy this new method of travel. Fidget moved smoothly, in spite of his age, and seemed to know by instinct whether the ground was rough or smooth and to test it before he trod.

It was warm, with a breeze that came off the land. The moors were still bright with heather, although the flowers were turning brown. A small bird flitted out of a bush, and disappeared into the undergrowth.

The path wound between the heather clumps, now high on the cliff, now dipping down, almost to sea level. Fidget suddenly stopped still, his ears pointing forwards, and a moment later Bracken too stopped, watching something in the grass.

"Lie down, Katie," Duncan said softly and the little bitch obeyed, her eyes also watching. She longed to chase but she knew that she would be in big trouble if she did.

Simon followed the line of the pointing ears and saw a weasel running through the heather, a small file of her tiny kittens behind her. She seemed quite unafraid, and came out on to the path in front of the horses, leading her family into the long grass on the other side. Simon counted three of them, following their mother nose to tail.

"The smell of the horses drowns our smell," Duncan said. "You see all sorts of things from horseback you'd never see if you were on foot, as the animals would scent you and vanish."

"Why did they ignore Katie?"

"Most of the hunting animals ignore anything that's lying still. They need movement to trigger their senses. A dog won't chase a cat if it freezes . . . silly cats run and then do get chased. That's why it's sensible to stand quite still if a strange dog comes up to you. If you run away you become a rabbit and it runs after you. If you make screaming noises you may make it bite, as you are making the kind of noises its prey would make. Stand still, act like a tree, put your hands behind you, your head down so you don't stare at it, and don't make a sound and most dogs will go away."

"Why not stare at it?"

"When dogs fight one another they try to stare one another down. A stare is a challenge, and also a threat. Stare at a dog and he might attack you, afraid you intend him harm. It's quite different to the long loving look our own dogs give us. The one that stops staring first may not get attacked as it has acknowledged it's the weaker. If they both stare and

46

neither give in, then they'll probably fight to try to find out which is top dog."

They had crested the little rise. The land in front of them sloped steeply down to the beach, and halfway down the hill, sheltered by a small rocky outcrop, was the tiniest cottage Simon had ever seen.

The old man who stumped up the hill towards them was also one of the oldest people Simon had met. Jock's hair was white, and thin on his head, his face craggy and wrinkled but his eyes were the brilliant blue of a summer sky when the sun was hot.

"Would you believe the old boy jumped the hedge?" he asked, as they came near. "Wouldn't have believed it only I saw him do it, and then he trotted off like a two-year-old, making for home. No way I could catch him. Glad to see you back, you silly old Fidget, you." He patted the wise head.

Simon was glad to dismount as he was beginning to feel a little sore and his legs ached. Jock and Duncan led the horses into the field and closed the gate. Duncan removed the bridles and blankets.

"I'm driving ye home," the old man said. "The Land Rover's playing up. Angus has just phoned. Morag has promised me a meal when we arrive and I'd drive to Peru and back for one of her suppers. Wonderful woman, your mother."

The old man led the way indoors. Simon, fascinated by Jock's accent, thought how odd it was to hear his grandparents called Angus and Morag.

He looked at the little sitting room in amazement. Three walls were covered with pictures of sailing ships, of galleons and clippers, of tall ships and small ships. There was a wonderful ship inside a bottle and on the table another bottle with a ship beside it, fully rigged, that didn't look as if it could ever go in. Then he saw the strands of cotton on the masts and realized that those would fold to put the ship inside and when the cotton was pulled away they'd rise in all their pride.

There were tiny ships made of ivory, of shells, of wood, on shelves that were ranged from floor to picture rail up the fourth wall of the room. Large paper swans hung from threads fastened to the ceiling and floated on the little currents of air that came through the part opened window.

"Those were sent me by one of the loveliest ladies I know," Jock said, seeing Simon looking at them. "They're trumpeter swans. She looks after them. She spends a lot of her time strapped to the wing of an aeroplane that skims over the Alaskan lakes, and brings out injured swans in a net. They take them to a special hospital to cure them."

"You're joking," Simon said.

"True as ye stand there," Jock said, putting the kettle on the stove in the tiny kitchen. "They give them medicine and massage to make them better."

"Massage? A swan?" Simon was sure he had come up against the world's best leg-puller.

"Like this," Duncan said, taking Simon's arm and rolling the sleeve up. He began to move his fingers in tiny circles that shifted the skin over the muscle. "Wonderful for sick animals and people with aches and pains. I met her here and she taught it to me. It helps horses get over lameness as well."

Katie butted against Simon's leg. He began to move his fingers over her skin in the way that Duncan had showed him. She stood quite still and then turned her head to look at him as if saying "Go on. That's wonderful."

"Ye can stop hiccups by doing those tiny circles over your middle," Jock said, producing strong coffee and a plate of jam tarts. "Only shop ones. I'm nae cook," he added. "Not got time anyway. Orders are coming in for the bottles."

"That's wonderful," Duncan said. "Many orders?"

"As many as I can cope with at the rate I work these days," Jock said, drinking his coffee noisily. "Used to be able to do two a day but I'm lucky now if I manage one in two days. Still, it helps eke out my pension and buys the jam and will buy food for Fidget and Bracken. Be nice to have them to talk to. Soldier's no company at all. Out all night and asleep all day, and never has time for anyone but himself."

Two green eyes suddenly opened on what Simon had thought a black sheepskin rug. Seeing no food was being offered, they closed again and Simon realized that there was a large black cat lying by the fire, blending with the rug itself.

Katie, coming into the room, walked over and sniffed him. Soldier opened one eye this time, recognized the dog and went back to sleep. She lay beside him, gold against the black, her tail wagging gently as she watched the three humans.

"At night, he's all hunter, fast and fleet and evil if ye're a mouse or a rat. By day he's laziness on four legs, and never moves," Jock said, but there was

49

amusement and pride in his voice. "One of the biggest cats I've ever seen."

He sighed again.

"I'd like a dog but my legs won't take me far, and it'd not be fair to have one I can't exercise. Don't grow old, young Simon. Too much time to spend remembering what ye could do once, and now take hours to do."

He stood up, cramming the last piece of a strawberry jam tart into his mouth.

"Come and see the lighthouse."

Simon thought they would be rowing out to sea, but instead the old man led him into a tiny conservatory, in which was a telescope.

It was focused on the distant white tower, standing on craggy rocks.

"Automatic now," Jock said. "No need for keepers. Three of us there used to be. I miss it. The wind and the roar of the sea, storm and calm, light and shade, and the green waters tumbling endlessly, hurling themselves against the rock. The gulls flying and calling, and coming in when we threw stale bread for them."

He sighed. "Ships passing, sometimes coming to grief. Migrating birds, often one of them falling exhausted so that we nursed it back to health, to continue its journey over the wild waters."

He laughed, an odd grunting noise that at first Simon failed to recognize.

"Never forget being out in our little boat one day. I'd coiled a rope in the stern and we'd settled down to eat our lunch. One of us on duty and the other two fishing. I'd just pulled in a nice fat mackerel when a pigeon came towards us, looking as if it would fall into the sea any minute."

He looked through the telescope and sighed.

'They were good days. That pigeon, she stayed on the rope for about two hours. Never blinking, just settled there, resting, trusting us completely. I put crumbs in front of her and she wolfed them down. Then she went. That night I went to get the rope to put away and discovered she'd left us a present. She'd laid an egg! Must have been uncomfortable flying with an egg inside her so she'd come to find somewhere safe to lay it.

"I miss the lamp." The old man sighed again. "Shining night after night, sending out its message to everyone who came near. Danger here, keep off. We polished it, took a pride in it. Took it in turns to cook. Not all the men were good at it. I wasn't. They had things on toast when it was my turn. Or eggs. Or omelettes. I can make those.'

He led the way to the tiny garage.

"My last stint was with Donald McKie. He'd once been chef in a fancy hotel for the tourists and he could cook like an angel. Fed like kings when Donald was there. He died last year. He's probably cooking food for angels now. Angel cakes." He gave his weird croaking laugh again.

It was a longer journey home, their route winding inland away from the path across the moors they had followed on horseback. Jock hummed as he drove, an endless tuneless noise, and didn't answer any questions if they spoke, his eyes on the road, which he

51

seemed to think might turn and attack him at any minute. Katie, at Simon's feet, leaned against his legs, blissfully happy to be with people and without her puppies.

The evening turned into a party, as Grandmother had prepared a feast, knowing that Jock fed sparsely when he was alone. They ate guinea fowl and roast potatoes, peas and carrots and cauliflower in a lemony sauce, with a blackcurrant cheesecake to follow, and lashings of thick Cornish cream that Grandmother made by heating a pan of Jersey milk very gently for hours over her stove.

"We want to camp on the island," Duncan said. "Before the weather breaks."

"I can row you across," Jock said. "You can camp right opposite my place, then you can signal to me when you want me to fetch you, or if anything goes wrong. Do this young lad good to have a few days in the open air and learn how to survive on camp cooking."

"Time to plan," Duncan said. "We'll make lists of what we need and take advantage of this warm spell. Be something to remember when you get back to the town and I'm cooped up in college. I'll miss this place."

He sighed. "I don't suppose I'll ever be able to spend much time here again."

"Nestlings fly," his mother said. "The old birds just have to get used to it, but we'll miss you both when you're gone. This place will be uncanny. So quiet."

Six more years, Simon thought, and then I'll be leaving home too, learning to live by myself. I wouldn't like to live here for ever, but I'd love to come back. It was odd to think of his parents living on their own and himself grown and working. I'd like to work with machines, he thought suddenly. Radios and fax machines. Maybe invent a new one that would make communication even easier.

He was fascinated by anything electronic, needing to take it apart and find out how it worked. That had helped him while he was recovering from his illness, as his father bought him kits to make up. He had made a bell that he could press whenever he needed his mother and a tiny radio set that did work, though he only managed to receive one station.

He had also built a model aeroplane and his father had promised him a kit for Christmas that would enable him to work it by remote control. He spent a great deal of time on his own as he was becoming afraid of other boys of his age, lest they all took to bullying him as They did.

Even now, although he was with other people, the memory of Them made him shiver and feel slightly sick. If only he need never go back to that school.

"Daydreaming?" Duncan asked, snapping his fingers in front of Simon's face. "Just to make sure you're there. I spoke to you twice."

"Just thinking," Simon said. "Nothing special." He was not prepared to share his thoughts with anyone. People so often laughed at his ideas. He wouldn't even tell them to Duncan, and he would never admit that he was terrified of them. He was ashamed of his fear.

CHAPTER 5

They had spent three days on the island. Simon, who had never camped before, marvelled at the ingenuity with which his grandfather and Duncan fitted out their site. They had chosen a hollow in the cliff, out of the wind, looking down on the beach, well above high-tide level. The tent was divided into two compartments, one for sleeping, one for eating. The little stove fitted neatly into a rocky recess, with no danger of falling over and starting a fire that would rage out of control.

Across the narrow stretch of water he could see his grandparents' home, as well as Jock's cottage, and yet they seemed to be remote, cut off from reality. Duncan, used to camping, produced meals that amazed his nephew. Grandfather said he was having a holiday and was on strike. He hadn't wanted to come at first but Grandmother had persuaded him, saying it was time he had a change and she could manage very well on her own for a few days.

The first three days had been halcyon days from a

land of dreams, where the sun shone and gilded the water, where a small breeze chased through whispering leaves, and they could swim and bask on the sands in the warmth.

On the fourth day Simon woke to a wind that screamed through the trees, tossing them as if they were slender saplings, and not the sturdy well-grown trunks that had weathered decades. He was not sure whether the gale had waked him or not. It was dawn. A grey light shadowed the world. The suck and swirl of an angry sea almost drowned the wind noise.

Tai was sitting erect, his ears pointing forwards, his eyes narrowed, intent on some sound that Simon could not hear. Beyond them, Shona, who had come with them to gain experience, and independence from her father, mother and sister, was curled against Grandfather, afraid of the noise. She had never known a gale before.

This world in which she had spent just twenty-five weeks seemed to her to have too many dangers. She hated raised voices, and the wind seemed to her a giant screaming its rage, so that she trembled when Duncan put her on her lead and took her outside. He reassured her, telling her that this was nothing to fear.

They woke very early on the island. It was just after 5 a.m.

Simon crawled out of his sleeping bag and dressed quickly. Outside the wind thrust against him so that he caught his breath. Tai, appearing briefly, yowled loudly and angrily and ran in again. He hated wind and rain, and wanted every day to be warm and sunny so that he could curl in a sheltered hollow and bask.

Duncan was still coaxing Shona who did not want to leave her sanctuary. There were devils out there screaming at her and she had no intention of facing them.

The birds were noisy, perhaps greeting the light, perhaps afraid of the wind, Simon thought, wondering how they could manage to fly, buffeted as they were by the giant invisible force that hurled the waves against the rocks, to shatter in spray that rose high into the air and crashed against the beach.

Excitement rode high. Simon was exhilarated, feeling more alive than he had felt for some months, fighting the wind that seethed around him and sounded like a hundred jet planes taking off, the very air vibrating. He left the camp site, walking towards the woods, lifting his face to the sky.

Dark clouds scudded across it, driven by unseen forces. There was a hint of rain in the wind, but there was light above the clouds and he did not think it would be more than a promise.

He wished they had brought Jansen, who was used to weather and would have taken this as part of living. Shona was too small and Tai loathed damp ground and rain and the unseen fingers that ruffled his fur. He almost went back for Duncan, but did not want to be thought a coward.

He walked along the little path through the woods. A rustle stilled him. "Don't breathe, don't even think of moving, or you'll see nothing. Be still as a statue." His grandfather's often repeated words were inside his head.

The leaves parted and into the shadows stepped a

roe deer and her two fawns. She raised her head, sniffing the wind, but it blew away from her and there was no hint of any danger. The little ones were twins, so like one another that no one could tell them apart. They came boldly into the clearing and began to play, heady with excitement generated by the wind, crashing after one another, round and round in mazy circles, first one leading and then both turning so that the other was first.

They were such delicate creatures, elf-like and unreal. He could have watched them for ever.

Behind him there was a soft warning bark. He turned his head, staring into the eyes of the buck that had come upon him without warning. Suddenly the buck twisted away and dived into the shelter of the bushes, followed at once by the doe and the fawns.

There was nothing left but the tell-tale tracks in the mud beyond him. He walked on. The light strengthened. There was a hint of sun shining behind the clouds. He was alone, miles from civilization. The trees surrounded him, and somewhere a branch cracked, broken off by the wind. Perhaps he would be safer on the beach. The noise deafened him.

He began to run, his feet making no sound on the soft ground. Through the woods and down the cliff path on to the shore, where the roar of the sea, as the angry waves crashed, was even louder than the groans of the crying trees. He heard the suck and swirl and surge of the waves on the shingle, saw gulls blown backwards, their cries borne seawards, as they wheeled and screamed and tried to fly inland, away from the turmoil.

Simon crouched at the edge of the narrow band of sloping shingle. Below it were jagged rocks, interspersed with long stretches of sand. The grass was sharp and spiky, unkind to bare legs. The tide was almost full but was still rising.

He heard a rustle behind him and cautiously turned his head. There at the edge of the woods were two badgers, returning homewards after a night spent hunting. A large male and a smaller, younger female. The grizzled boar moved ponderously, bear-like, while the little sow frisked around him.

The old male was seized by a sudden skittishness and butted her playfully, so that she lost her balance on the slope, rolling over and over, crying out in indignation, and then suddenly she was eager and filled with excited life. The two of them romped together, pushing head against head, rolling and shaking in delight. The dew-wet grass glistened and dampened their fur and Simon was so fascinated he almost forgot to breathe.

The male stopped playing and began to forage, his thick body almost dragging along the ground. The sow waited for a moment and then took the path to the woods. Sunshine, breaking through in a sudden gleam, revealed the brilliant black and white markings of her flattened head.

Her mate returned, carrying a small mouse in his mouth. He ate it, and then caught a shrew and killed it, but left it, knowing that these little creatures were not good to eat. He had been unable to resist the sudden movement. He disappeared into the wood and Simon walked over to look at the shrew.

His grandfather had once told him the story of the Shrew Tree in Carnforth, in Lancashire. Centuries before, a whole colony of the tiny animals had been trapped in the tree and died there. Farmers believed this gave the tree a special power and they took the twigs from it to strap on the back of sick cattle to heal them.

Duncan said that men used to hate shrews, believing that if one crossed your path you would die. There were people who thought that of owls too. Black cats meant good luck in Britain, but bad luck in Germany.

The wind was easing. Wind changed with the turn of the tide, Grandfather said. Here everything seemed to depend on the weather: on low tide, when the boats were trapped, unable to sail; on high tide, when they rode free and motored into the distance; on small winds and calm seas that were kind; on wild gales when the boats headed for harbour and sheltered until the weather relented. No boats would be at sea today. Nor could the three of them cross the water to the mainland, even if they wanted to. They were effectively marooned.

He crouched to look at a tiny beetle that was scurrying through the grass, its black body outlined in brilliant shimmering blue. A movement caught his eye. A tabby cat was strolling nonchalantly through the grass, some hundred yards away from him, making in its turn for the woods. Small-faced and dainty, she lifted her head. The wind blew from her to Simon, so that she had no fear. He flattened against the ground, watching. As she turned he saw the striped bushy tail.

A twig fell behind her and she turned fast, arched

her body and spat, a furious hiss, ten times louder than that Tai made when he was in a temper.

She appeared twice her normal size, a ridge of fur showing along her spine. The bushy tail was rigid. Simon caught his breath. This was no tame puss, walking in the early morning, but one of the Scottish wildcats. Fierce, Grandfather said, and dangerous, but only if you corner them. Leave them alone and they'll leave you alone. You might hear them. You'll be very lucky to see one. They're shy and they're wary.

The cat was unaware that she was being watched. She saw the twig and tapped it. A feather blew across her path and she darted after it, trying to catch it. She succeeded and tossed it and chased it again, playing with the wind, using it to enhance her game. She settled on a fallen log, savouring the warmth from the sun which was now stronger. Her amber eyes were slit-like. She kneaded the wood with outstretched claws.

She was on her way to her lair, a cranny in the crevice of the cliff, above the high-tide mark. She had borne a litter of four kits that year but now they were all grown and independent of her. She no longer had to hunt for her family, but could prowl and play as the mood took her and she was savouring her freedom.

The bugle call startled Simon, and then he laughed. Duncan was summoning him to eat. The wildcat vanished, and as she went an enraged cock pheasant, that had glimpsed her, yelled his gong-like warning. It was taken up at once by birds from far and near.

Cat, Cat. Cat. Danger. Danger. Hide.

There was a ghost presence as the cat showed herself briefly among the bushes. Simon watched her, a moving pattern in a dapple of light and shade, blending with the foliage, so that she was hard to detect. Then she was gone, hidden by thorn and bramble.

He was starving and anxious to tell Duncan and his grandfather of the creatures he had seen. He ran along the beach, his feet sinking into the soft sand beyond the shingle.

He made no sound, and the vixen did not see him. She had found a young pheasant, preening in the sun. He was unaware of danger. She began to clown, rolling over and over, and the bird stared at her. He was too young to have learned about foxes, and more stupid than most of his kind. He watched as she bit her tail, snarling, then spun in a circle, ending in a high leap, and sat, tongue lolling, looking foolish.

Over she rolled towards it. A step closer, and closer still. A leap through the long grass, her head high, her mouth open like that of a laughing dog. She stooped, creeping towards her prey.

Simon couldn't bear it. He stood up and clapped his hands. The pheasant flew. The vixen, baulked of her prey, snarled. She stared at Simon, one paw raised, her eyes glaring and then she too was gone and nothing was left but the memory.

He was sorry she was hungry but she would find new prey. The bugle sounded again. Duncan was becoming impatient. Simon ran over the short turf that edged the wood, unwilling to climb over the rocks that separated him from the cove above which was their camp site, as they were sharp edged, slippery and very dangerous. The wind raced alongside him, flattening the grass. The tide was on the turn, a faint border of wet sand showing that it was beginning to recede.

Tai came to meet him, walking regally, a king greeting his subject. Shona followed, a small whirl of excitement, her whole body wagging, her tail beating wildly, whimpers of delight escaping from her, behaving as if he had been away for ever. She picked up the lid of a saucepan that Duncan had left lying on the grass. Like all her breed, she needed to carry, and they had forgotten her toy rabbit, which she brought to everyone she knew.

"Food," said Duncan, producing a plate of bacon and egg and sausage and fried bread, rather like a conjuror taking a rabbit from a hat. "All the wrong things, but this life gives you an appetite. I could eat twice the amount I've cooked and so, I hope, could you." He took the pan lid from the pup and gave her a rolled up sock, which she took to her corner beyond the fire. She lay with her nose on it, watching them, hoping for a titbit from their plates.

Tai sat erect beside Grandfather, observing every mouthful. He was concentrating so hard that his blue eyes squinted.

Simon nodded, his mouth too full to answer. Seated cross-legged on the waterproof groundsheet his grandmother insisted he used all the time, he knew the world was a wonderful place, and that here on the island exciting things happened.

"I saw deer and badgers and a wildcat," he said, when he had cleaned his plate with bread to mop up the egg.

"Thought you might. So few people come here that they aren't nearly as wary as on the mainland. Didn't you hear the cats fighting last night? They made a tremendous row and Shona and Tai both came for shelter into my sleeping bag, scared out of their wits." Grandfather in his turn wiped his plate with a thick chunk of bread.

"Didn't hear a thing," Simon said. "I've never slept so well in my life as I do here."

"It's being out in the fresh air all the time and we have been pretty busy." Duncan poured boiling water into the washing-up bowl and dipped the plates. "If we did this properly we'd do all the washing in the burn but I did promise Mum we'd be hygienic. Don't want to send you back worse than when you came." He laughed. "Your dad doesn't think his young brother capable of being sensible. Don't want to prove him right, do we?"

"Three more weeks," Simon said. "Then you go to college and I go home. I wish we could stay here all the time."

"You'd soon tire of it," Grandfather said. He frowned. "The weather is one drawback. Suppose this gale goes on for all that time and we can't get food from home? We'll have to fish and trap and eat what's on the island. Our stores won't last for ever."

"It wouldn't go on for three whole weeks. You're having me on."

"I've never known it to, but you never know. There's always a first time." Duncan grinned at him. "Perhaps they could drop stores by helicopter if the wind weren't too strong."

Simon looked down to the water, now rough with white-topped waves that hurled themselves in defiance at the rocks. He was sure they were teasing him.

"Look," he said, and pointed, grabbing Duncan by the arm. "Look." Out at sea a small school of dolphins played together, their sleek bodies rising in graceful arcs from the water and landing with a splash. Simon was entranced, watching until they vanished and the sea surface was unbroken.

"You never think of them living their own lives, nothing at all like ours, until they surface," Duncan said. "Mum says life is to store up memories. I store up more here than anywhere else. They may call it Smugglers' Island but when I was small and we came here I used to think of it as Paradise Island. The old laird started a sanctuary here, which is why there are so many different kinds of wild animals. He brought them over and released them to live in peace, or as much peace as each will allow the others."

Simon watched the sea, but nothing moved.

"Let's tidy up and make everything shipshape. No use living in a mess. That's horrid," Grandfather said. "Chores to do before we go out. Tidy up. Roll up your sleeping bag. Wood to gather for the fire. Dog and cat to feed."

Had he been at home, Simon would have found the necessary jobs a bore, but here, in the open air, with everything improvised, he found them fascinating. He brought the last twigs to the mounting pile and looked at it in satisfaction. Enough wood here to keep them warm for a day or two. Shona took one of the bigger twigs and pranced round the clearing with it.

Tai, inspecting the grass, found a hole and stood by it, his nose down, his body eager, his tail erect.

Duncan laughed.

"He thinks he's found a mousehole. That's where I pushed in one of the stakes, till I found a better spot for it. It'll keep him busy for hours. He never leaves if he thinks there's a chance of a trophy."

Simon was looking at the far end of the little cliff. "There's a cave," he said. "Can we explore?"

"Lunch first," Grandfather said. "We might be living rough but we need to get our priorities right. We need to make plans. No use crawling into the darkness. That entrance tunnels deep into the island. We don't want to get lost."

Simon looked at his watch, unable to believe the various chores had taken so long. It was after one o'clock. He buttered the bread as Duncan cut it, and they made sandwiches from a tin of sardines and three scrambled eggs. The island was proving to be even more exciting than he had expected, and he wished that his companions would hurry, instead of stretching out after their food and lying with their eyes shut, savouring the sunshine. It was very warm out of the wind, and they were well sheltered, the sun reflected from the rocks. Tai lay on his master's tummy, purring, and Shona cuddled against Simon, and lay on her back with her legs in the air, a blissful expression on her face.

At last Duncan stretched and began to collect his gear. Simon watched as he packed two torches, a ball of twine, and extra jerseys into his little backpack. He added a packet of biscuits, a block of chocolate and a large packet of raisins, as well as the remains of the loaf, and knife and a block of cheese. Finally, Grandfather opened his eyes and stood up.

"Never does to go unprepared," he said, leading the way along the path. The black tunnel gaped open, diving deep into the hill, "Come on." Simon followed, but some of his enthusiasm had died. He thought he had never seen any opening that looked so uninviting.

CHAPTER 6

Duncan fastened the end of the ball of string firmly round a projecting spike of rock. Tai tapped at it, and tried to undo it, getting sharply scolded. Shona hesitated at the entrance to the tunnel and Grandfather picked her up and tucked her firmly beneath his arm.

The floor at the entrance sloped sharply, and then there was a sudden turn and daylight vanished behind them. The rocky walls were surprisingly dry, the torches angling forwards to show a curving passage that vanished into the distance. The floor was uneven, and in places was damp and slippery. Water trickled down the sheer faces of the tunnel, in places forming small pools that Tai lapped at, and then left in disgust.

The cat walked ahead of them, his tail erect, his body suspicious, as if expecting enemies to leap at him. He turned his head and yowled, loudly and often. Shona kept so close to them that Simon almost fell over her several times.

"We have to watch the levels," Duncan said. "It

goes down to below tide level and the other entrances flood. People have been drowned."

"Is it one of the old smugglers' passages?" Simon asked.

"You'll see."

They seemed to have been walking for ever, going downwards. Shona kept close to Grandfather's heels. She found a thick stick and picked it up and carried it, always glad to have something in her mouth. At home, the other dogs took her trophies from her. She suddenly felt more important and became bolder by the minute. She was the only dog, and she was the dog that carried things. Her small body began to swagger with pleasure.

Tai, still grumbling, walked ahead of them, tail erect. He hated the wet patches on the floor and shook each paw if he encountered water.

The vixen laired in one of the adjoining tunnels. Shona smelled her and walked closer than before to Duncan. Tai yowled angrily, recognizing the smell and hating it. The fox heard the cat, and retreated, not knowing what kind of danger threatened. Both animals heard the pad pad pad of her receding paws, but the three humans heard nothing and were puzzled by their pets' behaviour.

The tunnel opened out into a vast cave. Simon stared in amazement. There were benches round the walls, hammered out of the rock. There were recesses, in which all kinds of things could be stored. There was a winch and a pulley and a huge hole in the floor, at the bottom of which could be heard the sea. Simon kept well away from it.

Grandfather sat on one of the benches. Tai jumped up beside him and Shona lay at his feet. He produced sandwiches and cake and bottles of coke from his rucksack. Duncan and Simon explored.

"What is this place?" Simon asked. Light glittered on tiny crystals in the walls. A pile of old clothes lay in one corner and on one of the benches were two neatly folded blankets.

"It has a long history," Grandfather said. "It's been a refuge for people hiding from various forms of persecution. Roman Catholics hiding from Protestants and vice versa. Cavaliers hiding from Roundheads. Prince Charlie's men hid here, they say."

"Does someone live here?" Simon asked, looking at the blankets.

"Some cavers got trapped here once," Duncan said. "They left the blankets in case it happened again. If there are unusually high tides the entrance can be blocked for several days."

It wasn't a comforting thought.

Simon was hungry. Hunger was something new to him after weeks when he had felt food was the last thing he needed and everyone had been pressing him to eat. Grandmother's bread was crisp and crusty, the farm butter tasted wonderful and there were slices of home-roasted ham. They sat on one of the benches to eat. Tai and Shona watched every mouthful and ate happily if offered a tiny piece of bread.

"And smugglers?"

"You and your smugglers," Duncan laughed. "Yes, they were here. They unloaded at the bottom of the cliff and the winch pulled everything up to be stored.

It's been in use over the centuries, and was probably also used for contraband between the various wars that caused people to need to hide here."

"It's warm," Simon said.

"It keeps a very even temperature here, deep in the rock. There's signs of people having had fires here. I'd think there's enough draught to take the smoke away."

"I wouldn't like to have to live here," Simon said. "It's spooky and there are funny noises."

"Most of that is the noise of the sea, echoing and booming away down there." Duncan poured hot coffee from a large army flask into three mugs, and passed Simon a piece of apple pie.

"One of the most famous people living here was an old hermit they called Black Douglas. He had a black beard and a fierce temper." Tai came to Simon and put out a paw, trying to pull a piece of pie out of his hand. Simon broke a corner off and gave it to the cat. Shona promptly followed, coming from the edge of the torchlight, where she had been chewing a piece of roll, afraid that Tai would take it from her.

"Who was he?" Simon asked, feeding a morsel of his pie to the pup and hoping that ghosts didn't exist. The ghost of a bad-tempered man might be rather horrible.

Grandfather swallowed the last mouthful of his pie.

"A very unlucky man. He lived here just before the French Revolution. He lived on the mainland and had a pretty young wife and a baby girl. One night there was a tremendous storm, and his wife, coming up the garden with her arms full of firewood, was killed by a falling tree. He would have nothing to do with people after that. He moved over here with the little girl and saw no one. His brother used to row across with food for them, and leave it to be collected."

Simon looked at him, startled.

"What an awful life for a little girl. What about school?"

"I'm not even sure if there were schools in those days," Grandfather said. "If there were, I suspect they were run by monks or ministers, depending on who was in power at the time, and then only for the sons of rich men. Little Janet would probably not be taught at all even if she lived on the mainland." He paused to break off two large pieces of chocolate from a big block. "They say she had a dog that would do anything she wanted it to and two wildcat kittens and that she could tame foxes in the woods. She had a young falcon and she spent much of her time singing to the seals. She had a voice that could charm a bird from a tree, and the seals love music."

Simon thought of the child growing up alone on the island, with no company but the animals and a bad-tempered father who terrified people. Was he kind to her?

"What happened to her?"

"It's an often-told story," Grandfather said. "Repeated at the ceilidhs and even sung about. One day a young fisherman heard her and came to see her. He came again and again, but her father saw him and shot at him. He escaped. He came back some nights later and Janet joined him and they went away together. Black Douglas was completely unapproachable after that and terrified everyone. He shot at anyone who came to the island."

"What happened to Janet and the fisherman?"

"No one knows that either. They left the district and were never heard of again. Hopefully they married and made a good life for themselves. She deserved it after a start like that."

Simon looked thoughtful. It might have been fun for her, much more fun than a conventional childhood in a small cottage in a village. He wondered what it was like to live in a cave, with nobody else around. He would have hated it if he had to live there for always, but it might be fun for a few days.

"Time to go," Duncan said. "We have work to do before bedtime." He packed the debris from their picnic neatly into a bag and put it in his rucksack. Simon was very glad they had marked the way with string as several tunnels led into theirs and he would not have known which to take.

They came out into a wild afternoon with scurrying clouds and a crashing sea that sucked at the rocks. Somewhere in the woods a branch cracked off, sounding like a cannon shot. A bird, battling with the wind, hurtled about them, flying against the cliff, and fell at their feet.

Tai ran to it and Duncan called him off. Shona sat, looking, half-afraid.

The bird was a young kestrel. It had knocked itself out.

"We'll have to put it in one of the boxes to keep it safe," Grandfather said, tucking it under his jacket.

Simon was glad when they reached the camp site.

72

He was tired. Maybe he wasn't yet as well as he thought. He watched his uncle line a box with a spare shirt, and put the kestrel inside.

"It's not dead?"

Duncan shook his head. "We'll have to watch Tai. He's not very good with birds." He covered the box with a small blanket, leaving an air gap, and tucked it away inside the tent, lashing it firmly so that the cat couldn't get inside.

"What do kestrels eat?" Simon asked.

"Mice. Young rabbits. Insects. If it recovers it might eat some of the cat or dog food," Grandfather said. The afternoon had become chilly and he piled wood on to the fire. "It's time we had an early night. What shall we cook for our evening meal?"

"Stew with dumplings," Simon said, joking and sure that that wasn't possible. To his surprise Duncan produced a chunk of meat, onions, carrots and potatoes and set about putting them all into a big pan.

"Dumplings," he said, with a flourish as he put flour into a basin and added suet and salt and water. "Mum has always insisted all of us can cook and I don't want to live on boiled eggs and beans on toast for ever."

They left the pan simmering over the fire and walked towards the beach. The sun, as if to make up for the clouds and the gale, blazed down on them. They turned inland and climbed to the top of a little hill.

The island was so very small. A spit of land fingered into the loch. On the far coast the sea thundered on a rocky beach. Here the gap was narrow, the other side only a few hundred yards away. On the mainland, distant mountains rose in rolling ranges, changing shape as shadows raced across them. They were now near, and now far; now blue and now purple, now patched with sunlight on the fields that formed a checkerboard between grey stone walls that were only lines in the distance.

The mountains sheltered the island from the severity of mainland gales, but did nothing to stop it being battered by those that came from the sea.

At the top of the tide blue water lapped at every shore. At low tide the bare bones of the island showed and if the water went out far enough, ribbed sand lay at the edge of rocks pooled with water, and it was possible to cross, at the bottom of the tide, to the mainland. The traveller had to be swift and pick his time.

Herons fished, gulls haunted the pools hoping for flotsam and the bright sea wrack lay everywhere, patching grey rock and white sand with its orange clumps.

Duncan led the way down the slope. They walked quietly, making no sound. Once Simon stopped, and indicated a clump of purple orchids. They grew so freely here. He had never seen them before.

"Pyramid orchids," Grandfather said.

He glanced down the beach, and gripped Simon's arm, stopping him, and pointed. The wildcat was beside one of the small pools, her head, prick-eared, on one side. She was the largest cat he had ever seen, the sun glinting on her tawny tabby coat. Chin and chest were white, and the immense, bushy tail was striped with black.

She appeared to be intent on her hunting, but her ears moved backwards and forwards as she listened for sounds of danger, and her nose was busy reading the news on the wind. One movement to alarm her and she would be away, bounding lightly over the rocks, to dive deep into the woods and hide from danger.

She loved fish. She did not understand the movement of the tides and waves often chased her up the beach, but she learned to watch, knowing that when it was low, it left ridged rocks holding deep still pools. She could safely walk there then and hunt for food.

She crouched over a pool that held fronded sea anemones. Simon had seen them the day before. Some were small dark-brown globules, lying close against the rock, only opening to show their waving fronds when covered by water. Others were golden, or blue with red spots, or strawberry-coloured, waving fragile flowery fronds as they clung to the rocky ledges. She left them alone. She had learned, when a kitten, that they had sharp stings that hurt.

The three of them watched her as she sat on the rocks, delighting in the sunshine that bathed her fur and reflected back at her from the hard granite surface. Her tail waved gently as she gazed, wide-eyed, into the water, unaware of the watchers above her. Seaweed masked the depths, but she waited quietly and soon her patience was rewarded as a silvery shape darted momentarily into the sunshine and flicked a derisory tail before diving into safety among the weeds. She loved fishing.

Duncan lifted Tai and tucked him into his anorak.

Simon took hold of Shona's collar and held her still. They were well above the cat, on a little hill, but any sudden movement could alarm her.

There was very little noise. The sea soothed against the shingle, a small wind whispered over the weed and sighed in the bushes. Ears flattened, the cat poised herself above the pool, one paw dangling loosely over the rocky edge. There was a movement in the water, followed by the sweep of claw and a slash of silver and the fish was on the rock beside her.

As it lay, gills widening and shutting as it gasped, small mouth gaping, the cat patted the flailing tail. She spent a few minutes amusing herself as the fish twisted and jumped, trying to find its way back into the water. It was not the first she had caught and her hunger was almost satisfied.

But then the sight of food and the need to eat became more than she could bear, and she bit deep, killing. She crouched low, pausing to swear at a gull that dared to challenge her. He decided he had made a mistake and soared into the sky.

Duncan touched Simon on the shoulder and they slipped away. Tai was still captive in Duncan's arms and Shona followed Grandfather close, alarmed by the scent of the huge cat, and aware of danger should they meet her.

They walked quietly, making no sound. Suddenly a seal leaped from the water, slapping the surface, so that the sound echoed over the loch. Simon turned his head. The cat had gone, vanished as if she had never been. The rock on which she sat was empty.

The ground was spongy with bog moss. Duncan

bent to look at the earth at the side of the track they were following, and pointed out a tiny clump of flowers that Duncan said were also orchids. They looked most insignificant. Simon had always imagined that orchids were big showy flowers. The pyramid orchids were much bigger.

"Little bog orchids," Duncan said.

"Very rare," said Grandfather. "You're lucky to see them. I've only seen them three times before in my life."

The track led into a little wood that bordered the beach. No one had cultivated here for a long time. Trees grew thickly, their trunks slender as they fought one another for food and water from the ground and light from the sun. The undergrowth was dense, matted and tangled, and it was hard to find a way through.

Wherever there was a clearing, the ground was boggy, thick cushions of moss spongy beneath their feet. They stopped for a moment as Shona startled a young squirrel which was hunting the ground for food. The dog barked as the little beast raced up a tree, and looked down at them, chattering angrily. He ran along the branch, a small fluffy creature, his tail still rat-like, not yet come to adult splendour. He vanished in a hole in the trunk.

Grandfather and Shona settled on the grass. Simon stretched out beside them.

Duncan loved sketching. He sat, drawing large oaks with spreading branches, though none of them grew here. He drew narrow poplars and thicker cedars, ash trees, with bushes between them. Simon watched the busy pencil, fascinated. Duncan added a dot that was the squirrel, and drew tiny shrews, roe deer, and field mice.

"Time we went back to camp. I'm starving," he said at last, shading in the wildcat on her rock.

The wood gave way to a field, bordering the sea. Tai, released at last, darted through the grass and suddenly stood, his tail one big question mark and yowled loudly. Duncan and Simon ran.

The cat was standing beside a minute perfect dome made from broad-leaved grasses. He had parted the blades to make an opening and there, staring up at them in terror, was the tiniest mouse Simon had ever seen, four hairless blind babies suckling from her.

"Leave her in peace, you horror," Duncan said and picked up the cat who wailed and struggled, but was unable to move. Simon, glancing down again, saw that the little family was bedded on shreds of sheep's wool, carefully built into a mattress.

"She'll probably move her family to a safer place now," Grandfather said.

That night Simon lay listening to the sound of the sea, to the wind in the trees and thought of the tiny mouse making a new home for her babies, building it to withstand rain and gales, lining it to make it soft, hunting for strands of sheep wool caught in the brambles.

And then the long painstaking task of moving each baby, one by one, carrying them through the long grass which must seem like a jungle to her, and settling them safely, hoping that her deadly enemy would not find them again.

The mouse was no better off than he as she too had many enemies: cats and owls and hawks; foxes and weasels. He was helpless against his as there were always three of them, and They were all much bigger than he and could run faster. The world seemed a very scary place.

Tai, lying beside him, on top of the sleeping bag, twitched his paws in his sleep and Simon wondered if he were hunting in his dreams. When he fell asleep he dreamed that he was as small as a mouse and They were hunting him, making a great noise like that of a pack of hounds. He tried to run but his legs refused to move. He shouted in terror and was relieved when his grandfather moved close to him and held him in his arms, telling him to sleep again, nothing could hurt him here.

CHAPTER 7

The day was warm, the sky blue with streaks of hazy cloud. Simon was combing the beach for driftwood to mend the fire. Duncan was busy tidying up the campsite, and preparing their lunch. Grandfather went for a walk with Shona, who, heady with excitement, raced after seagulls, never learning that she had no hope of catching them, and Tai was exploring the rock pools and amusing himself with patting at the tiny shrimps that flirted through the water.

Simon walked over to the tiny jetty and stood at the end, looking down at the swirling water. The making tide carried dozens of jellyfish with it. Some were translucent, like white jelly, with four orange circles on their round bodies. The long filaments underneath them swung with the waves.

Others, bigger, carried beneath them the floating tangle of tentacles that Duncan said were lion's mane jellyfish. Conan Doyle had written one of his mystery stories about them. How did you write a mystery about jellyfish, Simon wondered.

No sense swimming with those around. He smiled as Grandfather came towards him and called Shona, leashing her, afraid she might dive into the water. The sting was remarkably painful and might well be fatal to a pup.

Tai, bored by inactivity, had strolled across to them. He patted Shona on the rump with a busy paw. She spun round to face him. He raced off. The two animals sped down the beach, first one and then the other being the hunter. Both Simon and Grandfather grinned as they watched them. Simon wished he could run as fast and had as much energy.

A caw attracted his attention. An old hoodie crow was sitting on a straggly bush at the edge of the beach. His ugly body was humped, outlined against the sky. He was very old and his mate had died so that this year he had been free of the hurly-burly life led by birds with young to feed. He had all the time in the world and he waited, bright eyes blinking, watching for an easy meal. He hoped the wildcat would come to hunt. She often left enough for him to eat.

It had rained the night before. Simon saw the cat's tracks in the mud at the edge of the path that led back to the camp site. He thought it likely that she would come that way again. Duncan said that most animals had a set routine. Old Jock had told him the story of a factory in the English Lake District that had been built on a deer run. Until the doors were put on, the deer, every night, went down the main corridor from one end to another, following their old paths. They were completely lost when the way was barred to them, and tried night after night to break through,

81

until at last they gave up and formed a new trail round the perimeter fence.

"Saw cat tracks at the edge of the path," he said to Duncan, arriving at the camp with his arms piled high with wood. He began to break the branches and add them to the blaze. Duncan had found a pile of old bricks and built a small enclosed fireplace, so there was no danger of flames spreading and the undergrowth catching fire.

"Need more wood," Grandfather said. "I'll help you."

Simon followed him down the trail. Shona ran ahead, and Tai followed, every now and then diving into the bushes to identify a smell.

"Tracks here," Simon said.

"That's not cat. It's otter. Look!"

A brown head was cleaving the water, leaving a white wake behind it as it swam. The little beast turned in towards the shore, and landed some distance away. Grandfather grabbed the cat and Simon took hold of Shona's collar. Both animals were impatient, wanting to give chase.

"Wind blowing from him to us, or he'd have smelled us," Grandfather said, under his breath. Simon knew enough now to be as quiet as possible and as still as possible. The otter was on a small sandbank just showing above the receding water, separated from them by a deep channel.

He was a young beast, only half grown. He ran along the sand, squealing shrilly with excitement. He loved shellfish and there were many cast up among the tangled weed. He was hungry, but not too hungry to play, and for some minutes he chased the sea as it ebbed, waiting until the new wave spilled over his paws before retreating, and running back again.

Grandfather handed Simon the binoculars and he watched as the little beast found the body of a sea urchin, dry and stripped of spines. He rolled it with his nose along a spit of rock, and tapped it until it fell into the sea and floated. He dived in, pushing it along with his paws. He grabbed it and lay on his back, holding it between his two front paws. It was brittle and he squeezed too tightly. He rolled over again and nosed the pieces, disappointed and puzzled by the fragmentation of his toy. He climbed on to a rock and shook his coat so that the bright drops flew, glittering in the sun.

A crab was scurrying sideways. He ran to investigate. He was alone for the first time in his short life and he had never met a crab before. He eyed it with interest. He put down his nose for a closer look and the crab raised angry claws and nipped viciously.

The otter sprang back, yowling, and rubbed at his sore nose with an urgent paw. He shook his head, bewildered by a creature that could deal such a painful nip. Simon grinned at his grandfather as he handed him back the binoculars.

"Could you see?" he asked.

"Most of it. Crab?"

Simon nodded.

"He won't tangle with a crab again," Grandfather said. "That taught the wee beastie a painful lesson."

The tide had turned and was beginning to come in. The otter wanted to explore. He swam to the beach,

83

looking up at the trees that edged it, so far away from them that he was almost out of sight. Just a small moving spot in the distance.

He began to climb the shelving narrow cliff. As he climbed a nesting gull saw him. Though her young were flown, she still came there to rest. He was invading her territory. She swooped at him. Her beak and claws raked at his eyes.

Upset by the sudden attack, he slipped and fell on to the beach again. The gull flew at him, and he fled to the sea's edge, the bird pursuing him, screeching like a demon. He dived off a rock into deep water, and she soared away, angry still.

"Nasty," Grandfather said. "Make a note. We don't go near that cliff or she'll be diving at us, and that's scary. She'll go for our eyes and could damage us."

Simon didn't like that thought at all.

The otter climbed out on to the diminishing sandbank again. This time he held a struggling dogfish in his mouth. He began to eat, but seemed, all the time, to be watchful, pausing between each mouthful to scan his surroundings. A gull flying ahead made him pause and stare anxiously skywards, but the bird flew on and he relaxed and began to feast again.

The sky was darkening, clouds forecasting rain.

"Let's get back to shelter," Grandfather said, releasing Tai, who pranced off, his tail erect, signifying his fury at being held too tightly and not allowed to chase.

Shona, who had settled to cuddle against Simon, happy to be in close contact with a human, trotted after the cat. They walked along the edge of the beach, taking the long way back to the camp site. The incoming tide brought bounty, as well as all the flotsam and jetsam and wreckage. There was driftwood in plenty and Shona, delighted with her freedom and the fun she was having on her own, without the other dogs to share it, picked up a large branch and trotted solemnly on, having difficulty in balancing it.

Grandfather, turning to look at the beach, nudged Simon, who turned his head. They were hidden now by the stunted trees. Tai and Shona, smelling the stew cooking on the camp fire, were running ahead. The otter had come back to the shore.

He was nosing among the seaweed and had found something that intrigued him. Remembering the crab, he was wary. He nosed it, but it made no move at all. It didn't try to bite him. It was quite solid and it resisted him, tangled up among the thick stems of the ribbonweed which hid it from sight.

It was nesting in a hollow in the rock. It mystified him and he pushed it. It smelled of the sea. There was a dead fish quite near it. The little otter pushed it with his nose and it rolled.

He growled.

The object fell on sloping ground and rolled again, towards the sea. The otter backed away, snarling sharply. It stopped rolling. He circled it warily and then sprang, convinced it was harmless. He patted it and it rolled across the beach.

"He's found a ball!' Simon said, laughing.

The otter ran after his find and caught it. He tossed it in the air and caught again in his mouth, then flung it from him and raced after it, repeating the action again and again.

He had never had such a game in his life. He crouched to regain his breath and let the ball go. It rolled towards the water and a wave, slipping over the breach, took it, and it floated away.

He ran into the water. He pushed the ball with his nose until he was able to swim freely. The beach shelved steeply and the sea was very soon deep. He rolled on his back, holding the ball in his forepaws, then tossed it in the air and caught it. Next time, he used all four feet to propel it skywards. It was spinning in the sun. He caught it and tossed it high again.

Like the urchin, it began to come apart. It was old and the sea had rotted it. It was too soft to stand such treatment for long. The otter was angry and his little sharp teeth savaged it, tearing it to pieces.

The sea took the remnants and tossed them back on to the sand. The otter followed and nosed them, but the game had ended and they refused to roll.

He climbed back on to the rock and began to clean himself, washing his face with his right forepaw, cleaning every hair and whisker. Satisfied at last, he prowled on, restless. He was thirsty after his food and vanished among the trees, searching for the little stream that wandered down on to the beach and fled across the sand at low tide.

Tai and Shona knew that he was hiding in a hollow tree on the way to their camp site. They smelled him when they passed, and Grandfather and Simon both wondered at their dedication to that particular place, returning again and again to sniff every inch of the ground around its trunk.

"They know things we don't," Grandfather said.

They spent the afternoon playing rummy in the tent, rain driving down, but by evening the sky was clear again and they lay in their sleeping bags with the tent flap open. Simon watched the moon swing across the sky and listened to the night noises. He was glad he was not alone in the tent. The presence of his grandfather and Duncan made him feel safe.

He thought of the otter, playing with his ball and knew that this holiday would be among the best he had ever spent and that he would never forget it. It was opening a door to a way of life that he had never realized existed.

Somehow They seemed very far away and much less frightening. Perhaps he would be able to stand up to them when he returned to school. He had put on weight since he came to Scotland. They couldn't call him skinny any more. Suddenly his jeans were too short, his shirts too tight and his shoes too small. Grandfather had taken him into town and bought him two completely new outfits. He woke once to hear Shona bark, answering the sharp yap of a fox. If only They could see him now.

CHAPTER 8

Day was only a rumour when Shona woke, barking.
Tai stretched himself and added his yowls to her din.
Everyone sat up, startled. There were heavy footsteps
outside.

"What on earth . . . " Duncan said, hurriedly putting on jeans and a thick jersey before looking out of
the tent flap.

A soft Scots voice spoke.

"No need to fear, little pup," it said. "We mean no
harm."

Grandfather put his head out of the tent and
grinned.

"Mac, where have you sprung from?"

Simon, dressing more slowly, went outside to find
the others deep in conversation with two men.

"Meet Mac and Andy," Grandfather said. "They
were fishing and brought us some of their catch,
thinking we could do with a change of diet."

"Morag keeps us in cakes and pasties," Mac said.
"She told us you were here. So this is your nephew,

Simon? How does it feel to have an uncle not much older than you?"

"I forget he's my uncle," Simon said, suddenly realizing that he was ravenous and wishing they could get on with breakfast. Mac was tall, black-haired, a giant of a man wearing a patterned jersey that stretched tightly across his ample chest. Brown eyes looked merrily out of a thatch of hair that hid the rest of his face.

Andy was smaller, spare-figured, his hair and beard less luxuriant, but a gleaming red that out-shone the sun.

"Where's your boat?" Duncan asked.

"Pulled high on the beach. Morag asked us to bring you back if you had had enough of rough living in the wilds. And if not, to bring news of you, as she is worried about the young one here, after his illness."

"Do you want to go back?" Grandfather asked Simon.

"No. I like it here. Can we have breakfast?"

"We've brought some of your granny's oatcakes to cook with the bacon; and fresh vegetables as well as the fish we caught this morning. Two lovely mackerel. And a sea bass."

"One lovely mackerel," Duncan said, looking at the cat, who had helped himself to the fish and was already gorging.

"We found a duck with a fish hook in its mouth," Andy said. "The poor thing was in such trouble we put it out of its misery. Would you like to share it with us this lunch time? Mac is a master cook."

Breakfast was eaten with more laughter than Simon remembered in his life. Both men were full of amusing tales, many of them of their own animals. Mac owned a lurcher that would steal the food out of a man's mouth, his owner said, and Andy had two Jack Russells that spent much of their time getting lost in rabbitholes, but emerging a week later as lively as when they went down.

They lived next door to each other in tiny cottages in the distant village, near the sea, and spent much of their time among their lobster pots. The beasts around them were more real to them than many of the people Simon met in his home town were to him. Each animal had its own characater, from the timid cat that met the fishing boats and daily stole his own dinner, to the bold lurcher that would do battle with fox or wildcat and never flinch.

To their pleasure, the two men decided to spend the day with the McGregors. Extra hands proved very useful collecting firewood from the woods and the beach. Shona, watching them, became self-important, swaggering along with her own contribution in her mouth, which she put carefully down on the wood pile. Tai explored the shore, hunting the rock pools but after two forays he curled up on Simon's sleeping bag and went to sleep. The fish he had stolen had filled him.

Simon, tiring, sat on a rock in the sun, revelling in the heat of the late summer. The trees were already colouring, the woods red and yellow and shining gold that reflected back the sun. Autumn came early here.

It was very quiet, and he was becoming used to being alone. Home seemed far away, an impossibly busy place, where there was always noise. Here today there was only the wind whispering in the trees, the soft waves breaking on the sands and the intermittent call of birds.

The tide was halfway, the rocks just exposed. One of the rocks moved and Simon realized he was looking at a seal. No, at two, at three, at four, and then, seeing a small form shift itself and wave a flipper, at five, one of them a baby.

Everyone else was busy at the camp site, stoking the fire, ready to cook the duck. Shona was with them, hoping that food might fall on the ground. There was no sign of life except for the wheeling, quarrelling gulls and one persistent youngster, in its baby brown plumage, still trying to convince its mother it was too young to hunt for itself.

It followed her everywhere, cheeping pitifully, until she lost her temper and chased it away, her beak stabbing relentlessly. The young bird began to turn the weed over, but it was not yet experienced and Simon saw it peck busily at a polythene bottle cast up by the tide. It seemed a remarkably stupid bird.

"We may as well take the boat out and try for more fish," Andy said, arriving so silently that Simon jumped. "Like to come? Lunch will be late, but we have little pasties to eat and a flask to drink from. Your grandfather thought you would be hungry."

Simon helped push the boat down the sand and then jumped in. Grandma's pasties, rich and brown, were filled with meat that tasted so wonderful that it lingered on the tongue and he longed for more when he'd finished.

The sun dappled the dancing water, and the fish seemed to be eager to take the bait. In no time at all they had two codlings, a haddock, two sea bream and two large plaice.

"Enough for us all and for your grandmother too," Andy said, as they pulled the boat well up above the high-tide mark and tied it to a tree. "Watch that cat of yours. A right wee thief, she is."

"He," Simon said.

"I call all cats she and all dogs he. Makes life easier," Andy said, though Simon couldn't for the life of him think how it did.

Mac made a stew from the duck, adding carrots, turnips, parsnips and potato. They ate it from bowls with spoons. Simon seemed to be permanently hungry. Grandma had sent several tins containing scones, home-made biscuits and one of her rich fruit cakes.

"Anyone would think we were staying for months," Duncan said, chuckling. "Mum is always sure we're on the brink of starvation."

They were so full after eating that they lay in the clearing in the sun, too lazy to move.

"Want to come and see what beasties walk abroad at night?" Mac asked. "Our wives aren't expecting us back till tomorrow. We said we'd sleep tonight in the cave. It won't be the first time. It's warm and dry down there."

They ate again at seven. Mac cooked the bream and then fried up the remnants of the lunch-time potatoes. Andy took the rucksack containing their sleeping bags to the cave while the others cleared up after their meal.

They sat and talked until the moon crept up the sky and a night owl called softly.

Duncan tied Shona to a stake inside the tent and put Tai into his basket and closed the lid. The complaints of both animals followed them, but died away when they realized no one was going to release them. They couldn't be trusted to keep quiet and would startle any creature that came near.

Simon, glancing at the shore, caught his breath. The sea had turned to silver, the edge of the beach was washed in silver and silver streaks shot through the water. Silver foam broke over black rocks. Out in the loch a boat sped along, the dipping oars sparkles of light. The wake creamed behind, glittering. Everything was alive with phosphorescence.

He remembered the night he had spent by the loch with his grandmother. The sea was a miracle of enchantment, unbelievably beautiful under the cold moon. An owl flew by, its wings silent, a ghost creature in a ghost world. Mac signalled with his hand and they all crouched. The wildcat was stalking down the glade towards them. Moonlight shone full on her thick sleek striped coat and on her bushy ringed tail, on her small neat face. She heard a sound, turned her head so that her eyes gleamed briefly and then she was gone, so fast that the glade emptied in a flash and nothing was left except the hooting owl, flying over again, mourning the lack of food.

The five of them crouched under the trees, as still as the bright stars that shone from a clear sky. There was a rustling on the hill as a big animal, unafraid, bull-dozed its way through the undergrowth towards them.

Simon saw the badger first. It was the boar, coming away from the sett, sniffing the air, striped muzzle lifted high, white bands conspicuous in the moonlight. He was very wary, his head turning from side to side, listening as he walked, and sniffing the air for news.

Simon's leg itched. An insect crawled over his face. It was almost impossible to keep still, but he knew that if he moved the badger would vanish as surely as had the wildcat. He concentrated on the entrance of the sett and saw the sow peer out cautiously and then climb from the opening and sit to scratch heartily, her hind leg thumping the ground. She vanished again and reappeared, walking backwards, clutching the bracken from their bedding to her.

She was followed by two cubs that began at once to play. They were tiny agile bears, excited by freedom, pushing against one another in their eagerness. The boar walked over to his earth pit, dug far away from the sett so that the nearby ground should not be fouled. On his way he caught an alien whiff, and when he returned, began to scout the ground.

The female brought out more bedding. She dragged it right away from the sett, and then began to gather fresh bracken fronds from the clearing.

The cubs rolled together, puppy-like, hissing and spitting, snarling at one another with an odd low sound, and then chased one another like school-children playing tig.

The boar found a young rabbit and killed it, sharing it with the cubs, who were shy of him. They had spent their first weeks alone with their mother and only recently met their father. He started grubbing for beetles, snuffling and grumbling, rooting them out to give first to one cub and then the other. The cubs, watching him, began to copy his actions and gained confidence, so that one of them snatched food from his jaws, and backed away in surprise when his father growled a warning to the little beast.

The wind rose and sang in the branches. The boar was bothered. He sniffed the air uneasily, lifting his head. Simon was sure they could not be scented as they were downwind, but something worried the animal. He began to root in the undergrowth. A moment later, he circled warily. He snarled at the sow who had come to find him and she, sensing his unease, shepherded the reluctant cubs back underground, snapping in fury at their heels when they lagged, unwilling to leave the excitement of wind and moon-shine.

The badger rolled. There was a sharp snap, and he stood, shaking his head angrily. He lumbered away and vanished. Mac waited until the rustle in the undergrowth had ceased and went to look in the bracken. Someone had set a spring trap.

They looked at it, wondering who had come to the island, who had intended harm. Simon felt uneasy, looking around him lest there might be an intruder there who would kill the badgers and might not hesitate to have a go at the humans.

They saw nothing more that night. Andy and Mac went off to the cave, and the three returned to the camp site.

They stared, appalled. Simon could not believe his eyes.

The tent lay in ruins, its canvas slashed through again and again. There was no sign of their sleeping bags. All the food had been thrown on the ground and stamped on, and battered cooking utensils had been scattered far and wide, flung by some unknown and angry hand.

They ran to the wrecked tent, hunting beneath the canvas. Tai's basket was open and empty. Shona's lead was still attached to the pole.

Grandfather began to swear, more angry than Simon had ever seen him. Duncan shone his torch around, picking up more and more mess. Simon stood helpless, not knowing what to do. Where were Tai and Shona? Had they been killed? Or stolen? He began to shake.

Grandfather saw his white face, and put his arms around him. Even so, every sound from the woods made Simon tremble. Who was out there? What kind of people? What further mayhem had they in mind? They had no food and nowhere to sleep, and no shelter.

"I'll kill them, whoever they are," Duncan said. "Raving idiots. Just let me get my hands on them."

Simon's feeling of security had vanished. Nowhere was safe, not even the island which he had thought too remote for anyone who meant mischief. This was wickedness, destruction for the sake of destruction. He felt as he did when he knew that They were stalking him, waiting round the next corner. Whoever had done this was as bad as They were, and They too might be hiding, waiting to leap out and pounce, eager to steal watches and money from his grandfather.

He tried to control his trembling, wanting to be brave, but he had never seen such chaos. He knew people were burgled, but only now did he appreciate the outrage victims felt as he looked around, seeing everything they owned destroyed, and, far worse, no sign of either the dog or the cat. Misery overwhelmed him.

Far away on the wind they heard the chugging of a small engine as a boat motored out into the loch.

CHAPTER 9

The full moon cast its light over a scene of devastation. Simon felt sick. What had happened to Tai and Shona? Had they been stolen, or hurt or killed? Or just set free? Andy and Mac were not far away and Simon and Duncan raced after them, arriving breathless, while Grandfather searched round the camp.

"Our camp site's wrecked," Duncan said, leading the way back. "Come quick." Andy and Mac raced back with them. The two newcomers stared at the devastation.

"Dear heaven," Mac said. "Who in the world – ?"

"Someone doesn't like you," Andy said.

Both men looked as shocked as the other three felt. Simon felt sick.

"Why? If they wanted to steal, why couldn't they just take things instead of leaving a mess?" Duncan was looking about him, hunting desperately for signs of the animals. Everything else could be replaced.

"They weren't thieving." Mac, who had been scouting around the site to see if he could find traces of either Tai or Shona, came back to them carrying three soaked sleeping bags. "These were in the burn. They intended to cause maximum damage. Probably to drive you away, and make sure you never come back."

Grandfather looked grim.

Nothing mattered now except the two animals. Where were they? Were they alive? What had happened to them?

"Shona," Duncan shouted. "Tai."

Only the echoes answered. The wind had risen while they were out and was roaring, bull-like, through the trees. The sky was darkening, clouds beginning to blow across the moon. Simon looked at his watch. Two in the morning. He longed to sleep, but sleep was not possible with the cat and the pup missing, and anyway, they now had neither shelter nor bedding. He shivered, chilled with misery and fear, not cold.

Who had been there while they were away? Who had been watching? If the animals were free on the island, they might meet the wildcat and fall victim to her raking claws. Or tangle with the vixen. They would be frightened. Simon prayed desperately that they had not been taken away, that they were not lying in the boat that had now vanished, not even the sound of its engine audible.

"Shona! Shona! Tai! Tai!" They were all calling, but nothing moved except the wind-tossed bushes and trees. They were shouting to the gale and only the gale answered them. Out at sea the waves were piling high. The loch was a bad place in evil weather and the night was no longer friendly, but fierce, challenging the puny humans who dared to try and live outside.

The moon would soon be covered by cloud, but as yet it shone bright and cold, revealing the smashed bottles, the food that had been tossed out and stamped underfoot, the pans with their broken handles, the shards of crockery. The empty basket and the cut lead that lay on the ground reproached them.

"We should never have left them," Duncan said, coiling the lower part of the lead and putting it in his pocket.

"How could ye know?" Mac was scanning the ground, finding only broken grass and heather. There were no tracks anywhere.

Forlorn, they walked towards the beach, not knowing where to look. The wind mocked them, so that they struggled against it and against the first thin fall of rain. Nothing moved on the marsh. Nothing walked near the wood.

The sea crashed against the rocks. There was no sign of movement anywhere. Simon felt as wary as a wild animal, expecting monsters to leap from the bushes. He kept close to his grandfather.

"We canna even fetch help," Andy said, as they walked towards their boat. "It is too wild to risk travelling on the water tonight."

Simon looked at the enormous waves and shivered.

"They didna intend us to fetch help." Mac's voice was furious, and he faced them with his fists clenched. "If I could lay my hands on them . . ."

Andy had left their boat upturned, well above high-water mark. There were now two large holes in the hull. The outboard motor had gone and the oars were broken.

They searched the beach, but when the moonlight died, there was no light at all. There was no trace of either animal anywhere.

Simon's fear returned. Fear of the dark and the wide open spaces; of the crash of the sea on the shore; and the sound of the gathering gale in the protesting trees; of the sting of salt on his face and the wind that pushed and thrust and shoved him so that it was difficult to walk.

"There is nothing for it, but to reach the cave and sleep," Andy said. "If we stay out here we will be exhausted and soaked. It will at least be dry."

They followed Mac and Andy along the shoreline towards the cliffs. The cave entrance was black and unwelcoming. They reached shelter, and the faint torchlight showed them that was all they had, for here too ruthless hands had scattered and tossed and broken. The lamps were lying on their sides, the glass cracked. The blankets had been slashed and the rucksack that Andy had left before they went badger-watching had been ripped open, its contents destroyed.

The sound of the sea was loud here, as if it were forcing its way up narrow passages, coming towards them. The wind echoed and screamed.

"We can do nothing till morning," Andy said. "We must lie close to keep one another warm. It will not be comfortable, but we have no choice. None of us has a change of clothing and it will be some time before anyone can send a boat for us."

"How will anyone know we're in trouble?" Simon asked. They had no food; the cave was their only shelter; everything they had brought with them had been wrecked. They had no boat. Old Jock was not due to fetch them until the end of the week. Another four days. The battery in the only torch they now had was failing.

"In the morning we will build a smoke fire, and old Jock will see it and know there is trouble," Mac said. All very well, Simon thought, but suppose old Jock was away from home, or had gone visiting his grandmother, or did not realize what their signal meant?

He could not settle. He lay curled up against Duncan, his grandfather solid and reassuring on the other side. Surely the four men could stand up against any intruders. He thought of Tai and Shona. There was so much that could have happened to them. He was sure he would never see them again, and lay wakeful and desolate, wishing they were safe at the cottage and had never come to the island.

Morning came at last. The wind still threatened them, and the waves crashed on the rocks at half-tide. Even the gulls had gone, and the beach was devoid of all life. It was a grey louring day, with a chill in the air. Simon and Duncan and Grandfather scoured the shore, calling. Mac hunted the woods, and Andy searched near the cave.

Hunger and cold added to their misery. Surely if the animals had been free they would have come back to the camp site? They never wandered. Humans were essential to both of them, and here, away from home, both had clung even closer than usual.

Simon longed to see Tai emerge from the trees, his black tail held high, his black legs covering the ground fast, his mouth uttering his constant yowl as he told them all that had happened to them.

Shona's little gold body would be close behind him as she raced to greet them, delighted to have found them again.

There was no sign of either.

Simon thought of the boat, chugging away. Were they there? Were they trapped, caught by the wind under a fallen tree? He suddenly remembered the old boar springing the badger trap. Were they in the woods, held remorselessly in iron jaws that would not release them?

They had given up calling, and searched desolately, sure they would find nothing. The sky was black, clouds banked more heavily on the horizon, threatening heavy rain. They gathered on the mainland, hiding the hills. At the far end of the loch, a mountain sprang straight from the water, threatening the island with its looming presence, but even that was shrouded in mist.

Even so, the sun rose behind the clouds, a sulphurous light streaking across the sky, colouring sea and woods with an eerie glow.

Far out, at the end of the loch, beyond the Isles of the Sea, beyond the Holy Isles, beyond Staffa and Iona, the Atlantic lifted itself into giant swells and the little boats fled for shelter. Even if they could signal, nobody could come.

Thunder rumbled, echoing and re-echoing from hill and hollow and rocky mountains. It reverberated, a continuous menacing growl that went on and on.

Lightning flashed on the horizon. Simon thought of little Shona who was terrified of noise. Grandfather had complained that she would be useless with the gun. She ran at even a shot from a toy cap pistol.

"Tai hates lightning," Duncan said.

Simon hoped they were in shelter, hidden from the storm. He couldn't bear to think of them crouched, petrified with fear, alone, soaked, listening to the terrible noises and seeing the terrifying flashes.

"Nothing for it but to shelter in the cave," Andy said. "Once those clouds loose their load, we'll be drenched in seconds."

The rain began as they raced along the edge of the beach. It poured relentlessly from a laden sky. Duncan, ahead of them, saw a crack in the cliffs.

He ran towards it, the others following him. The narrow shaft allowed all of them through and then widened suddenly. Andy shone his torch, revealing a cylindrical copper pot on a stand, under which were the ashes of a fire. Peats were stacked against the wall.

"I did not know this was here. And look, that is why we were unwelcome."

"What is it?"

"The remains of a still. They are making moonshine. Illegal whisky. They have cleared most of the evidence, but to someone who knows . . . "

"Who would it be?" Simon asked.

"Modern day smugglers. People from Glasgow – who knows?" Andy shrugged. "There's always someone prepared to break the law to make money."

"Suppose they come back and find us here?" Simon asked.

"No one can come to the island in this weather. Nor can we make a fire. None of us have lighters, and the matches at the camp site were thrown into the burn. Unless Duncan has some in his pocket?"

"I hadn't any need for them," Duncan said. "How can we let them know we're in trouble?"

"Andy and I were due home on the morning tide. Our wives will not worry about us while the weather is bad, sure we would not be fools enough to set out. But when the weather improves and we do not come home, then they will send out a search party. They knew we planned to spend only one night on the island with you."

The cave was small, but dry. Andy's torch, flashed briefly, to conserve the battery, revealed a shaft above the copper pot that went up to the sky, making a chimney.

They listened to the rumble on the hills, and watched the flashes lighten the dark, while the sea crept nearer, the suck and swirl drowned at times by the wind and the thunder.

Simon was glad that he was not alone. Storms in the town were frightening enough, but here, with the whole world raging with sound, they were terrifying. Speech was impossible. The wind drove through the gap, screeching, as if all the demons from hell were let loose.

Lightning dazzled on the peaks, sheets of blue and red and amber. The gap was lit by yellow forks that zigged towards the earth, a continual bombardment of electricity.

Simon thought of the birds and the beasts, hiding

under rocks and bushes, taking what shelter they could, exposed to the continual bombardment of light and sound and rain. Where were Tai and Shona? It hurt him even to think about them. He wanted to crawl up to his grandfather and take his hand. He wanted to be home and safe. He wanted to be anywhere but here.

He was cold and longed for fire; for heat, for warmth. He thought of log fires, blazing in giant hearths, of bonfires crackling, of their camp fire, only the day before, yet it seemed so long ago. He was hungry. Hungrier than he had ever been in his life. They had drunk from the burn, but had eaten nothing for over twelve hours.

Simon felt in his pockets. Not even a crumb. Not a sweet, nor a bar of chocolate. Maybe in future he'd never go anywhere without something to stay his hunger. He thought wistfully of his grandmother's pasties, which made his mouth water and his inside feel emptier than ever.

"The kestrel," he said, suddenly, in a lull in the storm, remembering the injured bird.

"That has gone too," Duncan said. "I went to look."

The wind died and returned, more frightening than ever. There was a rip and a sear of noise, and a crash as something on the beach blew against a rock. The sky was brightening, the clouds higher, and light crept into the cave, shining across the floor, glinting on the copper pot.

The rain was ceasing. The wind was dropping. The distant thunder was a low grumble, barely audible.

The five of them went to the shaft and eased themselves out on to the beach. Easy enough for Simon and Duncan, but both Grandfather and Andy found the space a tight fit and Mac, who was burly, had to struggle.

The air was damp. The peaks on the mainland were still shrouded by cloud. Simon, turning his head towards the beach, saw the waves worry a thick tangled mass of seaweed and driftwood, dragging it up the sand only to fling it high again and race away, returning in fury to snatch its trophy back and fling it on the water.

Grandfather organized them into a working party. Hunt up and down the beach and see what they could find. Perhaps there would be some sign that the two animals had passed this way. Look for tracks on the beach. Build a fire of driftwood. Maybe somehow they could light it, though nobody at the moment knew how. Anything to keep themselves occupied.

It was Andy who found the body of the kestrel, its neck broken. He hid it under seaweed, not wanting to worry the others. If the intruders could kill the bird, they might also have killed Tai and Shona. He rejoined the other searchers, his expression grim.

"We still have a useful tin opener," Duncan said, having salvaged it from the camp site. "You never know. We might find a crate of baked beans tossed up by the tide, from a wrecked ship."

"Maybe we can find some late eggs," Andy said. "We could eat them raw. Only it's a bit late for the birds to be breeding, so be careful; if there are any they may be addled."

Every tin in their store had been stamped on and thrust into the mud by the little burn. Mac and Andy had little food with them other than that supplied by Grandmother. What hadn't been eaten was useless, crushed by heavy boots.

"They must have had lookouts posted to watch for us," Mac said. "They needed time to do all they did."

"Maybe they got shipwrecked in the storm," Duncan said. "I hope wherever they are they're cold and wet, thoroughly uncomfortable and very hungry."

"I hope the police catch them and they're put in jail," Andy said. "They've cost us a mint of money. That boat of ours . . . "

Simon wondered if they ever would be found, and then knew that that was silly as Grandmother would soon realize something was wrong. People didn't die of starvation in a couple of days. It took weeks. For all that, he felt so hungry that he would gladly have eaten semolina pudding, which was served sometimes for school dinner and which he hated.

"You'll have a tale to tell when you go back to school," Grandfather said. "Not many boys of your age have been marooned on an island. Let's see if we can't find bounty along the beach. And we can watch out for Tai and Shona at the same time."

The tide was falling, leaving behind the debris of the gale. A line of sea wrack lay along the high water mark. Caught among it was the wreckage of a tiny boat, the name *Eileen* on one plank. Beside was half a barrel, stripped and empty, and beyond that, lying on its side, the humped shape of a dead animal, half-covered in weed.

Simon felt his throat thicken with terror. Was it Shona? Or Tai? He stared hopelessly, willing his feet to move and his mouth to open and tell the others what he had seen.

He had never felt such despair, not even when They were out to get him. Suppose the animals were both dead? He wanted to yell and scream and shout that life wasn't fair.

He pointed, unable to speak.

CHAPTER 10

Four pairs of eyes stared at the half-hidden shape and four pairs of legs ran fast towards it. Simon dragged behind. He could not bear to look. He dared not bend over the battered body, dared not face the reality that this was the end of a wonderful pet, that Tai or Shona lay there, beyond their help, beyond any help, broken by the wind and the tide and perhaps by the men who had wrecked the camp site. The seaweed covered rock as well as animal, and it was impossible to see properly. All they knew was that something lay there dead, so little of it showed.

Please, God. Don't let it be Shona or Tai. Please. Please. Please. He recited the words over and over like a litany, praying that this wasn't true, that he would wake up in his own bed, that none of it had ever happened, that they were not stranded on this unfriendly island, cold and hungry and wet, without hope of help for hours as yet, perhaps for days.

While the others bent over the forlorn body, he stared at the waves, at the rocks, at the distant mountains, now shedding their load of cloud. He wished it were yesterday, were last week, and that Tai and Shona were racing towards them, delighted to greet them, full of life and fun and excitement.

His legs dragged him reluctantly across the beach and he looked as Duncan stood up with a deep sigh, removing the seaweed that hid the body. A half-grown sheep lay there, most of it covered by the trunk of a small tree that had been uprooted by the wind and flung into the water, to drift with the tide. Only the head was visible.

"It must have been washed into the sea and drowned," Andy said.

Simon shuddered, his legs shaking with relief. He climbed the rock, bracing himself against the wind, his shoes slipping on the wet surface. He took them off. Better not fall and break an ankle. He needed to be alone, to hide the telltale tears that had come into his eyes, to gather himself so that the other four did not realize how near he was to crying.

He moved carefully. It was too easy to slide down the steep-angled granite into the deep water that lay, treacherous, on the other side. It waited to engulf him as it raged against the rocks. He left the beach, feeling it was safer in the wood. The other four followed at a distance, aware that their young companion needed to be alone.

Huge branches littered the ground, ripped from the trees above them. A giant elm leaned against the wind, its trunk creaking, its roots bared, the soil heaped against it. Here on the island trees grew tall, protecting one another, and untouched by man.

111

He looked for signs of two small animals, running through the wood, for the traces of paw marks on the ground. There was nothing but wet undergrowth and water dripping from the trees. The birds were stirring. Slowly, first one note and then another sounded on the air, voice after voice rising to swell the choir until the chorus of thanksgiving for the end of the storm rose above the wind noise and the woods vibrated with jubilant song.

Above them, fiercely warning, a magpie yakkered his danger call, and at once the note changed, to shrill chirp and sharp chik. Cat! Cat! Cat!

All five of them stood still, a wild hope starting. Was it Tai that was walking towards them, alarming all the birds? Hope was soon destroyed.

The wildcat came across the glade on silent feet. She crouched to drink from a small rill that sprang from the ground. Her ears were flat on her head, her lambent eyes watchful. A blackbird on a bush above her twittered his urgent warning for those that had not heard the magpie's cry. Simon had never been so conscious of wariness.

He could feel the alarm in the birds as they marked the cat's passing and twittered in fright. They knew she was coming, long before she came. A little bird told me. His grandmother said that to him when he asked how she knew something he was sure was a secret. Perhaps it was true, if you knew how to read the signs.

If you listened you could tell which way the cat was passing, and follow her by the urgent cheeps and yakks. Simon could not stand still any longer. He had to go on searching. It would be better to find Tai and Shona dead than to think of them lost and hungry, or stolen by men who might harm them and be cruel.

Not knowing what had happened . . . that was worse than anything he could imagine.

He did not care if he frightened the wildcat. He moved suddenly and she froze, staring at him, her lips curled back over her teeth. She leaped in the air, twisting, and was gone, melting into the undergrowth as if she had never been there. The bird notes began to mark her passage as she fled. They resented her intrusion, and, suddenly bold, they mobbed her, wings beating around her head, beaks stabbing, hoping for contact. The magpie flew at her, infuriated by her presence. The air was hideous with whirring wings and scolding tongues.

She took an undercover route to her lair, keeping to paths among fern and bramble. Slowly the anger died and the woods were still again except for soft calls of birds one to another, and the drip drip drip of the drops from the saturated leaves as the wind shook them.

Simon had almost forgotten hunger. He knew that the others were close behind him, following, wondering where he intended to go. They were all moving cautiously, knowing that if the pup and the cat were near, they would be terrified of people and might not recognize their friends at first.

He was tired. They seemed to have been awake for hours and hunting for ever. Wearily, acknowledging defeat, he sat on a fallen tree, and waited for the others to catch up with him. Andy, to his amazement, was carrying long fronds of sea kelp.

"Food," he said, in reply to Simon's astounded stare. "Beggars canna be choosers. It would be better cooked, but it's safe to eat raw and at least it is something to put in our bellies."

"It's not poisonous?" Simon asked doubtfully.

"Other nations eat seaweed as part of their usual diet. We eat laver. Seaweed's full of good nourishment, and the loch is clean water, not polluted like the sea around the coastal towns. Ye're not going to let those villains beat us and make us go under when we can keep ourselves alive and healthy without all the trappings of civilization?"

It was a long speech for Andy. Mac was already chewing at his frond.

"I washed them in the burn. Maybe they'd be better washed in the sea, and salty," Andy said with a grin, handing a piece to Simon. "There's many a shipwrecked sailor has survived on weed and what he can catch in the rock pools. If they don't come for us today we can go shrimping. Better to eat them raw than not at all."

Simon wondered what his mother would say if she saw him now, sitting in a wood, wet and cold and eating seaweed. She'd have a fit. A purple fit, he decided, wondering exactly how a purple fit differed from any other.

The seaweed tasted disgusting, slimy and fishy and cold all in one, but at least it filled the crack inside him and staved off the hunger pangs that had grown so fierce.

"I was in the army once," Andy said, "when I was not much older than Duncan. We did a survival course. They marooned us on an island much like this and we had to fend for ourselves for a week. Surprising what you can find to eat if you know how, and we had an experienced man with us to show us."

"Like what?" Duncan asked, hoping there might be an alternative to seaweed.

"There'll be bilberries if we go looking. And any number of leaves that you can eat raw if there's nothing better. It's not the best time of the year, as the young leaves are tastier, but you can eat the leaves of saxifrage, and oxeye daisy. Clover leaves too, though they taste better cooked."

"I'd like one of my mum's pasties," Duncan said, chewing hopefully and finding it hard to swallow. "You'd have to be very sure of your plants before you did eat them. I don't know sweet cicely from hemlock."

"Nobody teaches you youngsters anything of use," Mac said. "How many folk could survive if they were cast up here with nothing whatever to help them make a fire?"

"Not many," Grandfather said.

"If we had a fire we could live well. Worms make good food, and slugs and snails." He laughed at Simon's expression. "If you're hungry you'll eat anything to keep life in your body. You have to starve the worms for a day before you eat them. Then you squeeze them to get out the slimy stuff, and they're very good dried in the sun."

"What sun?" Simon asked, looking at the towering clouds that were banking up for rain.

Mac had finished eating and was looking around the glade in which they sat. He gave a sudden exclamation and went over to a tree. He dug deep into the hollow with his knife and returned to them, carrying a large honeycomb.

"I saw the bees. We can sweeten our leaves with this," he said, breaking off tiny pieces and doling them out to each of them. Simon luxuriated in the sweetness that filled his mouth.

"There are benefits to civilization," Mac commented, looking at his watch. "Battery-driven watches don't stop. Eleven o'clock. Another couple of hours before our womenfolk start to wonder where we are." He glanced out between the trees. "Wind's dropping and so is the sea. They'll be looking for us before nightfall."

There was a sudden bark.

Shona!

Simon turned his head and saw a startled roe deer with her fawn beside her, staring at him with immense frightened eyes. She turned and leaped away, the baby following her. He tightened his lips in disappointment.

The threatening clouds were breaking again, soft blue sky showing between long black streamers. The wind was high, shredding them into tatters and driving them along in front of it.

Out at sea rocks spiked out of the water, black and wicked with sharp teeth, death to any boat that ventured too near. The largest of them, a flat barren-topped island, no bigger than an ocean liner, was a bird sanctuary and its top was white with seething gulls, whose noise could be heard on the wind.

"The big rock is the Tiger; the little ones the Cubs," Mac said.

116

There were caves here too, cracks in the rocks and in the ground. Simon, walking towards the sea, heard a sudden soft bark, coming from below him.

"Shona!" he shouted, and his companions turned to stare at him and then they heard the answer, and immediately after it a long, plaintive, unmistakable yowl.

"They're there. In the caves. How in the world . . .?" But it wasn't important. They'd found them and they were both alive. The only problem was to get them out. Andy, casting his torch into passage after passage, saw only steep drops to the ground far below. Tai and Shona were trapped.

Simon, desperate to reach them, snatched Andy's torch and began to clamber over the rock.

"Careful," Duncan called. "We don't want to have to rescue you."

"This could be the back entrance to the smugglers' cave," Simon said. "Could we reach them if we went in there?"

"We need a proper rescue team," Andy said. "There's a maze of passages, some of them coming out at sea level, some of them flooding. No point in us all getting trapped."

"We can't just leave them."

Simon was casting around the rock. A fall had blocked the entrance to the largest cave, and when he called, the two voices answered him, sounding as if they were just the other side of the obstruction.

They must have wandered in from the other end. There wasn't a crack large enough to let any animal in at this end. They must have fled for shelter, and gone on running through the mazy dark.

Simon looked at the fall. Once there had been a slipway, up which a boat and its cargo could be dragged. When the tide was high there was deep water. There were iron rings bolted into the stone.

He climbed the slipway and looked more closely at the rocks. One of them was wedged across a gap that looked as if it might allow Tai and Shona to escape if only they could move it. He had not noticed that he was out of sight of the others, who were calling to him, scrambling to keep up with him, concerned lest he fall.

The rocks looked securely fixed, but Simon began to pull on one that protruded more than the others. He looked carefully at the stone wedged round it, afraid they might subside and crush the animals as they fell inside. Or he might bring rock on to his own head.

Reason told him he was being stupid, but the sharp insistent bark below him spurred him on. The rock twisted under his hands and slid away so suddenly that he shot through the gap, falling an incredible distance, sliding down the slope. He landed with a jerk that sickened him and looked forlornly up at the sky that showed so far above him.

His efforts had made matters worse. The others would be furious with him. They had no means of bringing him out. He was in a pit, the sides rising sheer above his head. He had fallen on soft sand, knocking his breath from him, but not otherwise hurt. There was no way of climbing out. He still had the torch, but the fall had broken the bulb. A thin shaft of sunlight angled into his prison, leaving most of it in darkness.

"Simon!"

"I'm here," he called, and was delighted to see Duncan's face staring down at him. A moment later it was replaced by his grandfather's.

"No bones broken?" he asked. Simon felt bruised, but was sure he had no major injuries. "Good. We'll soon have you out," he added, his voice reassuring, though Simon had no idea how that would be achieved.

"I fell on sand. I didn't know the pit was there," Simon said, fear beginning to surface. How *were* they going to get him out?

A moment later two small bodies flew at him, Tai brushing round him, weaving himself against Simon, purring at the top of his voice, while Shona wriggled and battered him with her wildly weaving tail, delighted to be with him.

"They're here, both of them. I don't think they're hurt," he said. "If they got in, I can get out."

"Ye canna risk exploring," Grandfather said. "Duncan and Andy are going back to the shore to see if anyone is coming yet. Mac has gone to see if he can find another entrance. We've no rope and it's a deep hole. From what I can see of it the sides are sheer."

"You won't go away? It's better now Shona and Tai are here, but it's scary and very dark away from the bottom of the hole. Daylight doesn't shine very far down here. There's a bend at the bottom of the slope."

He comforted himself with the thought that Mac would find the other entrance, or that a boat would arrive to rescue them, with rope on board. He wouldn't be here for ever. Tai cuddled up to him, wanting warmth. The air was chilly. Shona sat beside him, pushing her body against him, needing reassurance herself. She had been badly frightened by the men who had roared at her and chased her and Tai away from the camp, throwing stones at both animals. She had no intention of straying away from the only member of the family she could find.

"I'm staying here, to keep you company," Grandfather said. "Now don't do anything stupid. Just sit tight and we'll have you out in no time."

Simon very much doubted that but it was comforting to hear. He curled up on the floor, Tai tucked against him and Shona lying in the hollow made by his folded legs. He slept and woke, to hear an odd noise. Shona was nudging him violently, her small body trembling. He was lying in water. The tide had come in and their refuge was beginning to flood. There must be another exit to the beach. Perhaps if he had found it earlier he could have escaped, but it was no use thinking of that now.

"Grandfather," he shouted, and was relieved to see the face above him. "There's water coming in."

"Listen hard, Simon, and do as I say. Ye'll just have to take your life in your hands and go exploring. Look for a shaft that leads away from the beach. Make your way upwards all the time. Make sure you don't take any passage that leads downwards. The water is coming in through the tunnels. I didna think it would reach you, but looking now, it will. There's sea wrack growing by the entrance. The lower part of the caves do fill. I'd hoped you were above water level. I don't like it, but we've no choice. Andy came back just now to say that the only rope they had on the boat was cut to pieces."

Simon felt despair. There was nothing on the island that could be used to rescue him, and now he was in danger of drowning. The water, which had been ankle deep, was calf deep and rising. Tai was already making his way out of the pit, along a narrow passage that did indeed seem to rise upwards. Simon could hear the cat's yowl calling to him, leading him on.

Shona was at his heels, pressed against him, needing comfort, which he also needed. The water was now almost knee deep, coming in fast. They had to hurry. The light behind him faded and died and he was alone in the dark which surrounded him on all sides. There was no longer even the glimmer of light from the top where his grandfather had been sitting.

Suppose the men who had wrecked their camp site were here in the caves and the boat that had vanished across the loch had been nothing to do with them at all? How many were there? Had they left a couple of crew members behind? What would they do to him if they found him?

He thought of the wrecked camp site and the appalling damage that had been done, everything smashed into tiny pieces, ensuring its uselessness. What kind of people did that? The threats from the three boys who bullied him seemed almost insignificant. They had hurt and annoyed him but had never destroyed his property.

He had never been so frightened in his life.

CHAPTER 11

The dark pressed in on Simon, and the soft suck and swirl of the sea, coming closer and lapping round his ankles, terrified him. Tai was somewhere ahead. He could hear the cat's soft yowls. Shona was so close to him that she pressed against his leg.

Go upward, Grandfather had said.

He felt around in the darkness. Two sides of the pit were smooth and sheer, the third had a gap a few feet from the ground through which the water was pouring and he had to hurry. He was now wet as well as cold. On the fourth he found an opening big enough to stand upright. He couldn't see but he stooped and felt the floor. It was smooth rock. So smooth that he knew the water must come in here daily and creep its way through the cliff. In a few minutes that way too might be cut off.

If only he had a torch that worked.

No use worrying about that, but he did have Tai and Shona and Shona had a nose that could scent all kinds of things that he would never smell. Perhaps she could lead them to safety. Or was she too young to understand what needed to be done? If only he had Jansen who was old and experienced and would lead the way. Tai, ahead of him, was still grumbling to himself, trying to get away from the water that was wetting his paws.

The darkness was so intense that Simon felt he could touch it. He remembered a story of a man lost in a cave system who decided to find his way out by following a wall. He went on following it until he dropped with exhaustion. When he was found by his rescuers he discovered that he had been walking round and round an immense stone pillar, going nowhere.

They were climbing, Simon was sure. The path beneath his feet felt as if it were rising, and it was now dry. He could still hear the sound of water lapping behind him. He hit his head on an overhang and stopped, gasping with pain. The roof was lower, and he had to bend. Tai walked on, once or twice close enough to touch, but mostly well ahead, as if he were on a definite trail.

The walls here were smooth too and Simon suddenly felt that he was following a well-known route, travelled by smugglers long ago, bringing in their illicit cargoes. "Brandy for the Parson, baccy for the Clerk; laces for a lady, letters for a spy, and watch the wall, my darling, while the Gentlemen go by."

It had been one of his favourite poems. School seemed very far away and long ago. He had been blundering in the dark for hours, for years, for centuries. He reached out for Shona's head, for comfort.

The smugglers had horses, their hooves were padded with felt so that they rode soundlessly. Sometimes they covered them in phosphorescent paint, so that people looking out of a window would see a trail of ghostly riders, flying by in total silence, and turn away and hide in terror.

Nobody would ride a horse here. They would come with their load, with torches made of flaming pieces of wood, lighting up the passage, making their way from the sea shore to the caves where they stored the goods. He hoped there were no ghosts still walking these tunnels. There were sighs and moans made by the wind and the sea, and others that were unidentifiable. Fear walked beside him, drying his mouth and making him cling to Shona's collar.

The air was stale and smelled of fox. The fox would come to the surface, would hunt outside, would know the warrens and mazes. Maybe if he followed her smell . . .

Tai had come back to him, was weaving round his legs. Did that mean they had reached a dead end, that the cat could go no further? Simon had never known such darkness. In the far away world above him there was always a glimmer in the night, even when the moon was hidden. Here there was not even the ghost of a shimmer. Nothing relieved the blackness. It was total, tangible, terrifying, pushing against him.

He had no idea what lay ahead or where they would end. In another pit, the sides as sheer as that down which he had fallen? By a crack in the cliffs large enough to release the animals, but not large enough to allow him through? Or were they going downwards

124

again, towards the water, which might swirl and suck and fill the space and drown them all?

At least there was not silence. There was Shona whimpering now and then, Tai grumbling constantly, the sound of the sea behind them and the wind in the crevices. Where wind came, there must be a way to the surface. There was a crashing sound which, Simon realized with horror, was the noise of the waves breaking against the cliffs, finding their way inwards, ready to overwhelm them.

The roof was higher here and he could stand upright. He felt the floor. It still sloped upwards. He had been afraid of the wide open spaces but now he longed for them. This was imprisonment. There was a sick taste in his mouth, a thudding in his chest that was inspired by terror, by fear of the dark and what might lurk there, by fear of the sea, and its invasion.

He sat down and put his arms round Shona and buried his face in her fur. Tai crept to him, and leaned against him, purring, which seemed absurd.

Shona whimpered. He was holding her too tightly. He sat up and tried to think. Never give in to panic. Never give up hope. That was his other grandfather talking, his voice clear in Simon's head. His mother's father had been in a Japanese prison camp during the war. They had been beaten and tortured and starved, but they went on hoping, went on playing silly games among themselves, playing poker dice with inkspots on stones, running up astronomical gambling debts that were never intended to be paid, singing silly songs and making up idiotic rhymes about their captors.

There was a new sound and Shona crept even closer to him. The wind was rising, making eerie noises in the passages. If he could feel wind on his face there must be a gap that led outside. If only it were big enough. He stood up, and reached above him. The roof of the passage was high and there was no need to worry about banging his head.

At least the three of them were now out of reach of the sea. The floor was dry and dusty and the walls were smooth, without a trace of damp, except just once where a little spring trickled down them and made a pool at the bottom. Both animals stopped to drink. Simon licked the water that was running down the walls, but it had an odd taste and a trace of salt.

He was so hungry that he would have been grateful even for seaweed, and that had tasted horrible. The worry about the exit from the passage continued to niggle. There were so many possibilities. Smugglers' tunnels sometimes ended in cellars under old houses. The old house was a ruin, and fallen stone from the walls might block any exit.

Was it a natural passage or was it man-made? Either way, there might be roof falls along the way, and his exit would be blocked. Did it lead upward all the time, or was it going to make a sudden descent into an inland sea, where the water overpowered them?

Time had stopped and he had no sense of distance. He might have walked a mile or only a few yards. He wanted to shout, in the hope that one of the others might be near enough to hear, but he was afraid the whisky-makers might have come back.

He didn't know. He couldn't guess and maybe it was better not to think about that.

The dark seemed to gather and grow and deepen. He remembered being a tiny boy, lying in his cot, watching the scary shadows creep across the room. The dark of a winter night was never so deep as this. Nothing broke the blackness. Outside at night you could see trees and the etched solidity of buildings, and the glim on the horizon and the orange telltale in the sky from the street lamps in the town.

Light! Simon craved it even more than he craved food or drink. His eyes ached with trying to see. It must be terrible to be blind, never to see the shapes and colours of trees, or the ever-changing sky, or the pattern on the surface of a sun-dazzled sea. Never to know how people looked when they smiled, or know the gentleness of friendly faces, and the soft warmth hidden deep in a dog's brown eyes. Never to see how fur on a kitten blended softly and lay sleek or how food looked on a plate.

Steak and kidney, the pastry richly golden, with sweetcorn and mashed potatoes mixed with swede. Yellow, turning to brown, as his mother added gravy. Simon licked his lips. Every thought in his head led to light or to food.

He stepped carefully, one foot in front of the other, one hand feeling along the rough walls. They were not sheer, but sloped, sometimes tripping him, as a rocky outcrop barred his way and he had to climb over it. These were natural passages, not man made. Men would have smoothed away the barriers that half-blocked his path so that he had to squeeze himself

127

between them and the walls. Easy enough for Shona and Tai.

He had been climbing steadily, he was sure. Unexpectedly, Tai growled, a most odd noise, almost like that made by a dog, and Shona echoed the sound.

A thin wind riffled his hair. It was a gleam of hope. There must be a break somewhere, near to them. Tai swore, then hissed and Shona whined, as if she were terrified. There was a padding towards them of swift paws, large paws, and a fearsome panting. Shona cowered behind Simon's knees and Tai startled him by leaping to his shoulder and sitting there, close against his face, swearing steadily.

Simon crouched against the wall, unable to move, not knowing what was coming towards them. Enormous fox, or badger, or prowling tiger? Some demon beast from the realms of science fiction, lurking here for centuries, undiscovered by man?

It couldn't be a ghost. Or could it? Surely ghosts would move on soundless paws, not these thudding beats. The creature must be enormous. The padding sound came nearer, echoing eerily. His thoughts brought no comfort. This was how he had felt when he knew They were waiting for him, hiding round the corner, ready to pounce and mock and pinch and kick and hurt. He tried to still his mind and reassure himself, but all he could do was stand still and listen as the footsteps approached. Tai was swearing, a low continuous rumble and Shona was crouched flat against the floor, her nose pressed into Simon's leg.

There was a sudden flurry in the dark as Tai leaped. There was a howl of pain, as the cat had sunk his claws into the intruder. Shona was so frightened that she tried to creep into Simon's arms, burrowing against his chest.

There were yowls and hisses of fury from Tai and growls and sounds of pain from the unknown creature that the cat had attacked. Suppose the cat were killed? Brave little animal, flying to their rescue.

There was a momentary lull, and then another sound, that of heavy human footsteps, moving purposefully. Simon lay flat on the floor, too frightened to move. The vandals must have come back.

CHAPTER 12

Simon watched the path of light, and saw two hands lift the spitting cat, in such a way that the man who held him was not scratched. Tai, when put down, fled back to Simon, and jumped into his arms. Simon was trembling, unable to speak, knowing that this could not be any of his own party, as they had no torches. Tai was still rumbling, swearing furiously, his fur raised, so that he seemed twice his normal size.

The light dazzled him. He bent his head and put his hands over his eyes. Tai hissed again and Shona snarled angrily for the first time in her life. Simon held her collar. Who was this?

"Don't worry," said a pleasant voice with a smile behind it. "You're safe now. I met your grandfather. The poor man was desperate. I thought it better to come down here alone. I know the way well and it's never easy to lead another person. They're all waiting for you outside."

Simon felt as if he were in a nightmare, his legs like

jelly, refusing to move, but the gentle voice was reassuring.

"Don't be afraid of Landor. He was startled when your cat jumped him. He's as soft as a dog can be. He scented you down here. He's been telling me for some time that there was something unusual about. I didn't really know where to look. He always does."

The man turned the torch on his own face, shining it on blue eyes and a small fair beard and curling chestnut hair that clung to his head as a neat cap. The dog that was revealed a moment later was one of the biggest German shepherds that Simon had ever seen. He waved his tail regally, as he stood beside his master.

"I'm the new warden for the island. I only came here two days ago. I saw what happened to your site and was lucky enough, just now, to run into Mac and then Andy, who are friends of mine. You've had quite an adventure. Let's get you out of here."

"I was scared the men who wrecked our camp would be back." Simon suddenly felt safe with the big man beside him and the huge dog, even though Tai was still grumbling and Shona fearful.

"I don't think our unpleasant friends will return. They removed the still early this morning. I watched them. Binoculars are very useful. The police are on their track. I can contact my base by radio. I didn't realize you were all still here. I saw the boat arrive this morning and thought your friends had come to take you home. Luckily Landor told me there were people still on the island and we found them all worrying about you and trying to work out ways to rescue you.

131

He's a wonderful dog. I was going to start at the other end of the cave system but he insisted we came this way. I'd probably not have found you by myself. These passages are a maze, and lead off in all directions."

"I was scared," Simon said.

"Anyone would be. Let's get out of this warren. You aren't far from my home, and from there it's an easy walk to the outside world again."

"You live down here?"

"I'm not the first. By the way, I'm Jon Murray. Jonathan really but everyone shortens it. I met your grandfather, and also Duncan, very briefly, down at the shore.

"Did you know we were camping here?" Simon asked.

"Your grandfather asked for permission. I hadn't bothered overmuch with you, because I knew he would be sensible and not behave irresponsibly. I didn't know the still was operating until Landor found their hideout. Landor also found your ruined camp site. I waited for your return but as Mac and Andy were with you, I was sure you'd be leaving by their boat. I didn't realize those thugs had wrecked it."

He led the way through the passage. It was much easier to make good progress with the torch. Landor nosed Shona and licked her small face. She suddenly relaxed and trotted companionably behind him, completely dwarfed by his size. Tai preferred to remain safely on Simon's shoulder, grumbling to himself at intervals. He was an uncomfortable companion as, when he felt unsafe, he dug in his claws and he was remarkably heavy.

"You must be hungry. They spoiled all your stores, didn't they?"

"I'm starving. We ate seaweed. It tastes disgusting." Simon made a face at the memory.

"It's not too bad cooked. Health food shops often sell it. I enjoy it for a change. Not as a staple diet though, and I prefer it dried. Some of the Japanese weeds taste interesting."

Simon had been following the torch's beam.

"Here we are. I told your grandfather I'd feed you and get you warm before we met them. I took them matches so that they can build a fire and cook some sea bass I caught this morning. They won't be worrying about you now. I knew Landor would find you."

Simon, recovering from his terror, looked around him. The cave was surprisingly roomy. It was fitted out like a bed-sitting room with bookshelves, a small portable table, two comfortable camping chairs, and an inflatable bed in one corner, with a sleeping bag and pillow neatly upon it. A grate in one corner blazed merrily, woodsmoke scenting the air, reminding Simon of bonfires in the autumn gardens at home. A chimney made of a metal that looked like tin led through a crack into the open air.

"No one can see the smoke from the mainland," Jon said.

Hurricane lamps gave ample light. Simon looked hungrily at a trestle table loaded with all kinds of food stores.

Jon Murray laughed at his expression and took a bar

of chocolate off the table and threw it to him. Shona saw the dog's bowl on the floor, half-full of food, and raced towards it. Tai leaped off Simon's shoulder, reaching it first, eating hungrily. Shona whimpered miserably.

"Poor little girl. Bet you haven't been able to catch a rabbit or so down here, have you?" Jon said, and filled another bowl with dog food from a sack in the corner. Landor sat beside his master and watched them benevolently.

"Lie down, Landor," Jon said. "They must be starving and you're not."

He threw the dog a bread roll and then cut four others into halves, filled each with slices from a chunk of corned beef that stood on a plate, underneath a metal cover. He added chutney, and handed two to Simon, eating his own as he worked. He filled a small knapsack with bread and butter and rolls and two more tins of the meat, adding a can opener. Cakes followed, and more bars of chocolate.

"First aid for hungry refugees," he said. "The bass were very small, and won't go far with four big men." He looked at Simon's wet clothes.

"Have to get you out of those. Mine will drown you, but with my shorts and a very thick jersey you ought to be warm, at least," Jon said, handing Simon a towel. Simon put down the uneaten roll and stripped off by the fire and dried himself. The water pouring in through the gap in the cave wall had soaked him from the chest down. Jon grinned when the boy was dressed in clothes that swamped him. It was wonderful to be warm and dry.

The warden led the way through a second opening

134

into a wider tunnel, Landor following him. Tai and Shona had emptied their plates, and, anxious not to be left behind, raced after Simon.

"We're well above sea level here," Jon said, as they walked past rough rocky walls that seemed to enclose them too tightly, so that Simon longed for air and room to move and distant spaces. He would never be afraid of the moors again, he thought. Anything was better than being imprisoned down here in the dark.

"Do you like living underground?" he asked.

"It's warm, it's dry, it's out of the wind, it's free, and it's comfortable. I'd have to build myself something if I stayed up top, or else live in a tent. It's much cosier down here when the wind's blowing and the air's chilly. It's not very different from being indoors with all the curtains drawn. The air's fresh too at this level. There are all kinds of cracks and crannies that lead outside."

"I don't think I like caves," Simon said, wishing their walk would end.

"I love them. I used to pothole a lot, exploring all kinds of underground systems, all over the world." Jon shone the torch in front of him. "Some are fascinating, especially when you have stalactites and stalagmites and wonderful rock crystals that glitter when you shine a torch. Others have the most marvellous drawings of animals and hunting scenes from prehistoric times."

"I don't think I ever want to be underground again." Simon felt happier with the torchlight, but his memories of the dark and his fears of being drowned were too recent.

135

"I'm used to it," Jon said. "Not very far now. There's a little hollow out of the wind just beyond the end of this passage. They're waiting there. I persuaded them not to try to hunt for you themselves. It's too easy to get lost and nobody had any light. It was a good job Landor found them when he did as your grandfather was about to explore and I feel sure he would have got lost. He was very worried, knowing you were alone in the dark and that you might not be able to find a way out."

"Are there so many passages?" Simon asked.

"It's a network of tunnels here, a few of them man-made, leading back to the cellars of the old house," Jon said. "I learned my survival techniques when I wasn't much older than you. My father loved caving too."

The passage twisted and turned and suddenly opened out into a wider tunnel, ending in a glare of light so fierce that Simon had to shield his eyes. The sun blazed out of a blue sky.

"Take your time," Jon said. "It's surprising how quickly our eyes get used to the dark and can't take bright sunshine."

Moments later they were standing on a small pinnacle, looking down at the beach and the sea below them. Simon thought he had never seen anything so wonderful in his life. Blue waves dancing, flecked with light, white birds swinging down the sky, calling to one another.

He was aware of patterns in the rocks that he had never noticed before, of the rough grey-green grass that bordered the beach, and clumps of pink and blue and yellow flowers. He smelled woodsmoke and cooked fish, and then they rounded a buttress of rock and came on the rest of their party. Grandfather took hold of Simon and held him tight, as if he'd never let him go, and the others sat and grinned, relieved to see him safe.

Shona rushed round everyone, wagging her tail and barking, and then picked up a thick stick and walked around with it. Suddenly there was a party atmosphere.

"Jon said he'd bring food, so we didn't save you any bass," Mac said.

"If I'd known I was going to have company I'd have caught far more. It was only a mouthful," Jon said.

Mac threw more wood on the fire, making it blaze. Duncan gripped Simon's hand.

"OK?" he asked.

"I am now," Simon said.

Jon had produced a billycan from his capacious knapsack and the water in it was nearly boiling. He had polythene beakers and plates, and handed them round, together with little sachets of soup.

"Instant food," he said, grinning. "You should have heard my dad on that. Nothing like that when we went camping. We had to do everything the hard way. Spoiled, we are now."

Nothing had ever tasted as wonderful as the soup and the rolls that went with it. Simon had never been so hungry in his life, in spite of the food Jon had already given him.

"A feast for a king," Andy said, devouring roll upon roll, as well as cake and biscuits. Landor lay at his master's side, watching every mouthful. Shona, still hungry, snatched at Simon's roll and ran off with it. Tai put out an experimental paw and hooked food from Mac's plate.

Simon looked down from his seat on a large boulder towards the sea. The sun had gone, and clouds were masking the blue. The small waves were strengthening as the wind rose, and sang softly in the trees.

"Watch," Jon said suddenly, and took a notebook from his knapsack. The rock twenty feet below them moved suddenly revealing a large seal. Beside her, hidden up till now, was a well-grown pup. He frisked at the edge of the water, playing with a long frond of seaweed which he teased in his mouth and allowed the sea to take and then pulled it back. His clumsy gambols alerted the dogs. Jon leashed Landor, and Duncan held Tai, while Andy took Shona by the collar.

"They're grey seals," Jon said softly. "They're bigger than the common seals. That little fellow weighed about thirty pounds when he was born. He'll be around ninety now, in all probability, if not more. They grow fast."

He handed Simon the binoculars and Simon looked down at a round furry face with enormous dark eyes, and black whiskers. Shona, frustrated at being held, barked, and at once mother and baby were on their way to safety in the sea.

There was a seething movement, a slide and slip and flurry and a slap and splash as the other seals slid into the water. Simon watched the pup's head as he

138

swam through the waves, his wake creaming behind him. He somersaulted twice, delighting in movement, as frisky as a young lamb.

They made for the open sea. The heads vanished and the loch was deserted, as if they had never been. Nothing moved in the water. It was impossible to believe the seals had ever been there, or that the deeps hid so much life.

"How big is the island?" Simon asked. "I thought it was very small."

"About seven miles long and four miles wide. I haven't had much time to explore, as I was busy setting up my camp in the cave. I had to carry everything from my boat and it took ages. There are a surprising number of caves underground. I don't think I've found all of them yet, by any means. Landor found the cave with the still in it by accident the first night we were here. Luckily the men weren't there."

He stretched himself out, and took another roll.

"We must have been at the other end of the island, or inside the cave when they attacked your camp site. Landor would have heard them if we'd been near. He might have given them a bit of a shock. He's a trained protection dog."

Tai, now used to Landor, was nosing around. He suddenly tapped at something that crept out of a hole in the ground. Simon caught a glimpse of a long sinuous shape in the grass.

"Tai's got a snake," he shouted. "He'll get bitten."

Mac went over to the cat and lifted him up. The snake wriggled away.

"It's a slow worm. They don't bite," he said. "It's not really a snake, though it looks like one. It's a lizard."

"Lizards have legs," Simon said.

"This has the remains of legs under the skin. Snakes don't. They've lost them altogether. Its eyes and tongue are like lizards, not snakes." Grandfather was watching, his eyes amused.

"It's very bold," Duncan said, watching the wriggling creature which had not gone far.

Mac walked over and picked it up.

"It left its tail behind," he said. "The clever wee beastie will grow another. It uses that as a way of defence. Tai was left with just the tail and the rest of the creature is safe in hiding."

The afternoon was warmer than any they had yet had, the sun brilliant in a blue sky that was reflected in the waters of the loch. Simon rolled over, and looked out to sea.

"Boat coming," Andy said a moment later. "It looks like the *Mairi Meg*. Old Jock and Hamish Grant will have been sent to fetch us."

"I radioed to tell the police about the still and the vandalized camp site," Jon said. "They'd contact your homes to find out if you were back yet and realize you were marooned." The boat was as yet merely a speck in the distance. They watched as she turned and nosed her way towards the land. She anchored in deep water, and within a few minutes a rubber dinghy was launched from her side, and the little outboard began its welcome putter.

"Thought we'd lost you," Old Jock said as he

landed. "The police told us that your camp site had been wrecked. Jon reported it. Your grandmother's nigh out of her mind lest they hurt you too. Alex Grey and Sandy Wiley. Villains both, and they have been hunting them for a long time. Spiteful, and wicked as well. The police have them safe. Caught them with the still in the boat and a nice cargo of firewater with them."

"We'll be glad to get home,'" Grandfather said. "Simon's had enough adventure to last him a lifetime. I never bargained on anything like this."

Jon grinned as he said goodbye.

"Come again," he said. "I can promise you a quieter time next holiday. Or have you been so frightened that you never want to come back?"

Simon looked at the island, lying quiet under the sun. No one would ever guess that it had been the scene of so much terror.

"I'll be back," he said, and intercepted a glance between Duncan and his grandfather that puzzled him, unaware that they had detected a new confidence in his voice and in the way he moved.

The dinghy was too small to take all of them. Old Jock ferried Grandfather and Simon and the animals back to the boat, and Hamish returned for Mac and Andy and Duncan.

The *Mairi Meg* was dancing on the water, and was suddenly full as everyone came aboard.

Jock turned her nose for home. Simon watched the island recede. He felt years older. He had grown up in the past few days. He had overcome his fears. The animals were safe, and so was he.

Everyone was waiting for them. His grandmother, and Mac and Andy's wives and children; Jansen and Katie, and Emma, and the cats. The kittens had grown and were tumbling over one another, thoroughly in everyone's way as they all watched the boat nose her way in to the little jetty.

Simon thought he had never heard such a din. Dogs barking excitedly, cats wailing, Tai answering them at the top of his voice, everyone shouting eager greetings to them as they came ashore. His grandmother hugged him tightly.

"I don't know what your mother will say," she said, hugging him to her and then leading the way indoors, where the women had been busy all morning preparing a mountain of food. Robert Graham, the local policeman, was there too, wanting to know what had happened on the island.

"You did well," he told Simon, who felt a small warm glow of satisfaction.

The immense meal that followed was a celebration for a safe return, Grandmother said, enjoying the company and delighted to be able to prepare food for so many again.

They ate their way through pasties and pies, through ham and salad and potato salad, with cakes and cheesecakes to follow and ice creams for the little ones, who raced around shouting, and went outside to clamber over the walls and run on the beach, the tide now far out.

"Better than seaweed," Mac said, laughing, as he cut himself an enormous slice of veal and ham pie.

That night, lying in bed, about to go home in a few

days, Simon thought of school. He had so much to tell his friends. He had done so much more than his enemies had ever done. Suddenly They seemed unimportant.

He fell asleep and dreamed that the three monsters were waiting for him. He waved a hand and they turned into brown rats and Tai appeared from nowhere, chasing them until they were out of sight. The cat yowled, and he woke to find the Siamese sitting on his chest, regarding him intently. He tapped Simon's cheek gently with his paw and then snuggled down in the curve made by his knees as he bent them.

Simon thought of his enemies and grinned suddenly, knowing that the nightmares were gone, and that when he went back to school he would be able to stand up to anyone. No one would bully him again.

He stretched and turned over and fell asleep and this time he dreamed that he was walking with Shona and Tai on a sandy beach, and the seals were coming to greet him.

When he woke, he washed and dressed and flew downstairs and out into the windy morning, racing across the shore with the dogs. He knew he now loved the wide open spaces, the rolling waves, the sands below the rocks that bordered the beach, the island across the water, lying placid under the sun. He had so many memories to take back with him.

His grandparents watched him, smiling.

"They'll never know him when he goes home," his grandmother said. "He's a different boy."

Simon, seeing them standing in the doorway, waved and yelled a greeting, and then raced back to them, the dogs spilling round his legs. Life would never be the same again and he knew now that no matter how bad things were, he would find a way out of his difficulties. Fear could be conquered. He looked back at his timid self, wondering, and then went in to deal with the huge plate of egg and bacon and fried bread that his grandmother set before him.

"Ready for school?" Duncan asked, busy with his own packing.

Simon stood against the wall, noting that his head was at least an inch higher than when he first came. It was level with the light switch and had been below it. He had grown so much in those few weeks.

"I can't wait," he said.